Willow took a deep breath, sketched in the air with her hands, and muttered perhaps four words in what sounded like Greek.

Buffy felt a wave of absolute, bone-chilling cold push past her, and she shivered.

The door turned to ice and there was a crackle and pop as the electricity running into it and around it shorted out. Willow swayed slightly, but her arm shot out and she leaned against the wall. Buffy and Xander both moved to steady her, but she shook it off. Oz moved around them, closer to the door. The werewolf's growling grew louder and more menacing.

"Oz," Buffy said.

The wolf turned, black lips curled back from gleaming teeth. She saw no human intelligence in his eyes, but she knew that he at least partially understood what went on around him.

"Giles is mine."

## Buffy the Vampire Slayer™

Available from ARCHWAY Paperbacks and Pocket Pulse

Available from POCKET BOOKS

# THE LOST SLAYER

## Part Four

## Original Sins

## CHRISTOPHER GOLDEN

An original novel based on the hit TV series
created by Joss Whedon

**POCKET PULSE**
New York   London   Toronto   Sydney   Singapore

For information regarding special discounts for bulk purchases, please contact Simon & Schuster Special Sales at 1-800-456-6798 or business@simonandschuster.com

Historian's Note: This serial story takes place at the beginning of *Buffy*'s fourth season.

This book is a work of fiction. Names, characters, places and incidents are products of the author's imagination or are used fictitiously. Any resemblance to actual events or locales or persons, living or dead, is entirely coincidental.

An *Original* Publication of POCKET BOOKS

 POCKET PULSE, published by
Pocket Books, a division of Simon & Schuster, Inc.
1230 Avenue of the Americas, New York, NY 10020

™ and © 2001 by Twentieth Century Fox Film
Corporation. All rights reserved.

ISBN: 0-7434-1188-9

First Pocket Pulse printing November 2001

10  9  8  7  6  5  4  3  2  1

POCKET PULSE and colophon are registered trademarks of Simon & Schuster, Inc.

Printed in the U.S.A.

# Previously, on <u>Buffy the Vampire Slayer</u> . . .

*A new breed of vampire arrived in Sunnydale, faster and stronger than others of their kind, and with a kind of magickal energy surging inside them. These are the Kakchiquels, vampire servants of the ancient Mayan demon-god called Camazotz.*

*Buffy had recently come to believe that the only way she could be content in her life and still be an effective Slayer was to separate the two halves of her life completely, as though Buffy and the Slayer were two distinct people. That meant trying her best to keep her friends out of her life as the Slayer, to handle those duties all by herself. But having the best of both worlds soon proved more difficult than she had expected.*

*Even as she began to learn more about Camazotz and the Kakchiquels, and to attempt to locate the demon-god's lair in Sunnydale, Buffy was visited by the ghost of former Slayer Lucy Hanover, who brought a warning. An entity of the spirit realm, a clairvoyant being called The Prophet, had predicted that Buffy would soon make a mistake that would have catastrophic results.*

Before she could follow up on Lucy's warning, the search for Camazotz heated up when it was determined that his current lair was probably a ship moored on Sunnydale's coast. Despite Buffy's desire to handle it on her own, Giles insisted that it would be faster to have Willow use magick to locate Camazotz and that they would attack as a group, given the gravity of the threat represented by the Kakchiquels and their master. Buffy was supposed to have Willow gather the ingredients necessary for the spell and then the two of them were to meet Giles in Docktown, the run-down section of Sunnydale where the town's shipping industry is concentrated. But when Buffy called Oz's looking for Willow, the young witch was not available. Though she left part of the message, Buffy chose not to tell Oz about the spell, the ingredients, or the planned rendezvous, hoping Willow's absence would cause Giles to abandon the search for the night. She planned to then search for Camazotz on her own.

But Giles was not deterred. Over her protests, Giles and Buffy went together to the harbor master's office, hoping to discover some hint of strange goings-on that might indicate which ship Camazotz was using as a lair. Giles insisted she stay in the car.

The harbor master turned out to be a vampire in service to Camazotz. While Giles waited and Buffy grew impatient in the car, the harbor master informed the demon-god of their arrival. Buffy realized things had gone wrong and broke into the harbor master's office to find her former Watcher in the clutches of that vampire. Then Camazotz and a group of his Kakchiquels appeared, and the Slayer was faced with a terrible choice. If she fought, Giles would probably be killed. If she surrendered, they would both likely die. Knowing that the first rule of slaying is to stay alive, and reasoning that Camazotz would keep Giles alive to use as bait to lure her, she fled the scene.

Later she and her friends tried to determine the location of Camazotz's lair, now desperate to rescue Giles before it was too late. Willow summoned the ghost of Lucy Hanover. The spirit indicated that The Prophet's visions had grown stronger. Fearing that The Prophet's dire predictions may have something to do with her current predicament, Buffy asked Lucy to see if The Prophet would speak to her. When the dark, sinister apparition known as The Prophet did appear, she revealed that Buffy had already made the mistake and that the dark future she had predicted could not be averted. She offered to let Buffy see this future, which she claimed she could do if Buffy let her into her mind.

But The Prophet was not what she seemed. In truth, she was Zotzilaha, the estranged bride of Camazotz, fleeing from her mate in spirit form and searching for a powerful host body with which to defend herself against her husband. Zotzilaha had come to Sunnydale to possess the body of the Slayer, and Camazotz had come in pursuit of his errant bride.

When Zotzilaha touched Buffy, she invaded the Slayer's body and forced Buffy's soul out. Through magick whose nature has yet to be revealed, Zotzilaha *pushed Buffy's soul forward in time five years, into the nightmare future she had warned the Slayer about.*

*The soul of Buffy-at-nineteen was merged with the soul of her older, future self. In that dark future, Buffy found herself in captivity. Years before, the Kakchiquels had captured her and chosen not to kill her, so to avoid the rise of a new Slayer.*

*Buffy eventually escaped and found that vampires now controlled all of Sunnydale and its surrounding environs, their influence spreading with every passing day. She made her way south out of Sunnydale, where she linked up with representatives of the Council of Watchers. The Council had set up a base and a large force of operatives to thwart the reign of the vampire king she had heard rumors about. Among those operatives were her old friends, Willow, Xander, and Oz, all of whom had been changed by the hard years since they last saw Buffy.*

*Willow then revealed the most horrifying truth of all about this terrible future—that the king of the vampires was Rupert Giles.*

*In the ensuing days, Buffy became a part of the Council operation, even as she dealt with awkwardness in the rebuilding of relationships with her old friends. During that time, the headquarters was infiltrated by the vampire known as Spike, who had been employed as an assassin and enforcer by Giles. At Giles's behest, Spike had killed Buffy's mother and Anya, among others.*

*Spike had suspected that the vampire king had been aiding Buffy since her release, that he somehow hoped to win her over rather than destroy her. When he challenged Giles with that theory, furious that Giles's indulgences had led to the death of his beloved Drusilla, the king threw him out a window into the sunlight in an attempt to kill him. Enraged, Spike had come to find Buffy before leaving California so that he might share with her all he knew of Giles's grand plans of conquest. In that way, he hoped to have his vengeance on the vampire king.*

*Buffy and the others captured and interrogated him, took the information he had to offer, and then they dusted him.*

*Now aware of the speed with which Giles's plans were moving forward, the Council had no choice but to hurry its own schedule along. Their forces were broken up into units, and a massive assault was launched upon Sunnydale the following sunrise.*

*The objective of Buffy's unit was to infiltrate Giles's lair in City Hall, eliminate the vampire presence within, and to destroy the vampire king, once and for all. . . .*

# CHAPTER 1

"All right. Let's go."

Buffy led the way down the corridor toward the stairwell that would take them to the basement of City Hall. She quivered with an electric awareness of her surroundings. Of all the horrors she had faced in her time as Slayer, it was possible that as a vampire Rupert Giles was the deadliest, not due merely to his cunning, but because Buffy loved him.

It was broad daylight outside, the midmorning sun glaring down upon the town as squads of Council operatives attacked nests of Kakchiquels, the vampires who were loyal to Giles. Communications had been silent with other units for several minutes as the operation unfolded in earnest. Buffy had helped to formulate the plan, so she knew that the nests would be burned where possible and the vampires attacked one-on-one only where necessary. The numbers were against the Council, but the sun gave them the edge they needed.

Or at least that was the hope. Buffy had a feeling that it was going to be a closer fight than any of them had admitted. If she could dust Giles, however, that would be the end of things. Without the vampire they looked to as a king, the Kakchiquels would lose their cohesion and it would be every leech for himself, the way it always was before Giles came along.

When they had stormed City Hall, Willow had used magick to burn some of the Kakchiquels. The flames set off the sprinkler systems on the first floor of the building and Father Christopher Lonergan—who was both a Council operative and a Roman Catholic priest—had spoken the words to the penitential rite, turning the spray into holy water. Vampires had screamed and run but the water was everywhere and it made their flesh bubble and steam and finally disintegrate.

Lonergan was a psi-operative who had a specialized ability to psychically sense the presence of vampires. Now, upstairs, he led the rest of the unit through City Hall in a room by room search, exterminating vampires as they went. They would work their way up, and inform Buffy immediately if Giles was located.

It was just the four of them—Buffy, Willow, Xander, and Oz—but that was okay. Once upon a time, she could remember having thought that in order for her to be an effective Slayer, she had to learn to operate on her own. Now she realized how foolish that was. This was the way it was supposed to be. This was right.

With the fire alarms blaring and the sprinkler system on, they passed right by the elevator banks. A red EXIT sign ahead marked the door that led to the basement. Buffy didn't even bother trying the knob. She popped a side kick at the metal door, right beside the knob. Metal shrieked and tore and it banged open.

With a quick glance upward, Buffy started down toward the basement. Oz followed right after her; the werewolf sniffed the air and the stairs as they went. Willow was behind him, and Xander covered their flank. He had the crossbow dangling from a leather strap around his shoulder, but he let it hang there as he pulled a nine-millimeter Glock from its holster at his side.

At the bottom of the stairs was another door. A huge letter B was painted on the wall, but other than that there were no markings. No guards. Nothing out of the ordinary at all. Buffy paused on the last step, feeling the damp heat of the werewolf's panting breath on her back. Oz sniffed several times in quick succession and began to growl low.

Buffy nodded. "I smell it too," she said.

"What?" Willow asked.

"Don't even know what to call it," Buffy told her. "Static. Like the bug zapper in Xander's backyard."

"Electricity," Willow said, her voice a sort of hush.

"Exactly."

Willow stepped past Oz, studied the door for a moment, then glanced over her shoulder at Xander.

"I'm a little tired already," she told him. "Catch me if I fall."

"Always," Xander replied without emotion. It was a simple statement of fact.

"Hey," Buffy said. "I can do it if it's too much—"

"No," Willow said quickly. "We need you in front. Just be ready."

A small smile flickered on Buffy's features. "No such thing. But let's do it anyway."

Willow took a deep breath, sketched in the air with her hands, and muttered perhaps four words in what sounded like Greek. Buffy felt a wave of absolute, bone-chilling cold push past her, and she shivered.

The door turned to ice and there was a crackle and pop as the electricity running into and around it shorted out. Willow swayed slightly, but her arm shot out and she leaned against the wall. Buffy and Xander both moved to steady her, but she shook it off. Oz moved around them, closer to the door. The werewolf's growling grew louder and more menacing.

"Oz," Buffy said.

The wolf turned, black lips curled back from gleaming teeth. She saw no human intelligence in his eyes, but she knew that he at least partially understood what went on around him.

"Giles is mine," she said.

Then Buffy took a deep breath, faced the frozen door again, and leaped at it in a high drop kick. The ice shattered into a million shards. The door was gone. They were in.

The basement was dark save for the amber glow of emergency lights on the walls. Clearly this was not Giles's lair. There were other corridors that led to this place, doors on the other side of the vast chamber in the basement, but this was the main room. Once it had undoubtedly been a massive storage area of some kind.

In some ways, it still was.

Half a dozen Kakchiquel sentries, their eyes blazing orange in the darkened room, looked up and snarled in alarm as they entered. But the sentries could not keep them from seeing what lay in the basement.

Bats hung from the pipes that ran all across the ceiling. On the floor beneath them, shackled and chained to iron rungs sunk deep in the concrete, was the god of bats, the demon Camazotz. His green, pocked flesh was obscenely bloated, like a leech that had feasted until it was ready to explode. The demon-god's withered wings were barely visible underneath its grotesque bulk. Around the swollen, distended demon, seven vampires were latched onto his putrid flesh, sucking at him like newborn kittens, crackling with the energy they siphoned from the captive demon's blood.

Buffy shuddered, stomach convulsing at the sight. "Now *that* is really gross."

At the sound of her voice, the suckling vampires glanced up, mouths smeared with demon blood. The sentries surrounded them. Camazotz began to cry out in a high, keening, lonely wail that sent a chill through her. The god of bats, she realized, had gone insane.

Xander stepped up beside her. "Giles isn't down here. Let's make this quick."

The vampire sentries rushed at them, eyes blazing, fangs bared.

"You read my mind," Buffy told Xander. A part of her wanted to warn him, to warn all of them, that the demon energy coursing through the Kakchiquels made them stronger and quicker than average vampires, but she thought better of it. They knew, after all. They had been fighting Giles's minions for years.

"You dare?" one of the sentries snarled, fangs bared as he lunged for her.

"Yeah," Buffy replied curtly. "We dare."

She had her sword in a scabbard slung across her back, but did not bother to reach for it. Once she had used that same sword to draw Angel's blood. Only recently, Giles had slipped into the Council headquarters and brought her the sword as a gift, as though daring her to kill him with it. Buffy would use the sword when she had to.

But she did not have to just yet.

She ducked under the vampire's outstretched arms and shot a kick up at his chin. Her heel connected and the impact shook her bones. He staggered, but only barely, and his eyes blazed and sparked even brighter. In an elegant, murderous ballet, Buffy took one step out from in front of him, then whipped her leg around again in another kick that cracked the back of his skull, knocking him forward. She slammed her stake through his back with enough force to separate the bones and push through to the heart. He exploded in a cloud of dust.

"We dare," she whispered to herself.

All around Buffy, her friends moved into action with a fluidity that exhilarated her and shamed her all at once. The four of them moved so well together, and yet she could not help but recall the days when she had attempted to push them out of her life as the Slayer, as if she had suffered from multiple personalities of a sort; as though she could truly separate Buffy from the Slayer. Ironically, it was that very attitude that had led to her present predicament, with the soul of her nineteen-year-old self thrust into the future and now sharing the body of a Buffy who was five years older.

They made her proud now, her friends, so that she could barely imagine going into a major conflict without them at her side.

Willow sketched sigils in the air and snapped off shorthand incantations in ancient tongues with an air of confidence Buffy herself envied. Her red hair was tied back in a long ponytail that swung with every graceful movement. A wave of cold slivered across the room as one of the sentries turned to ice. Another burst into flame, the blaze hungrily licking at his clothes with a low roar of fiery consumption.

The seven vampires who had been suckling at Camazotz's flailing, pustulent body had begun to come out of the daze of contentment they were in. They seemed almost bloated themselves now by the power they had leeched from their former master, now simply their battery. Buffy had always wondered where the demonic energy came from that had enhanced the Kakchiquels, gave them their additional speed and strength and the electric fire in their eyes. Now she had seen firsthand.

The feeders, surfeited upon the power of the god of

bats, thrumming with that dark might, moved to join the sentries in battle against these intruders.

Gunshots punched the air in the basement, and Buffy could feel the subtle changes in air pressure against her skin and her eardrums. The bats hanging from the pipes all along the ceiling shrieked at the loud noise and some of them took flight, but settled again seconds later.

Buffy spun to see Xander firing again and again into a pair of sentries with his Glock. The bullets wouldn't kill them; he was using the gunfire to hurt them, to set them off guard. Then he slid the gun into the oiled leather holster and snatched up the crossbow that hung from the strap across his shoulder.

There was a roar off to Buffy's left and she whipped her head around quickly, expecting an attack. But it was not one of the remaining vampires who thundered with such savagery. It was Oz. He tore the head off a sentry as Buffy watched, bone and flesh ripping with a sickening noise, and then the vampire crumbled into gray soot. The werewolf moved on to the vampires who had been feasting on Camazotz, claws flashing and tearing.

Two of the feeders leaped across the air at her and Buffy dodged. In her life, she had never been in better physical condition. Her muscles rippled as she moved with the deadly precision of a scalpel. With a flurry of blows, she kept them both off-balance for several vital seconds. One of them, a pale blond female, became so enraged that she simply reached out for Buffy's throat.

The Slayer let her come, felt the vampire's grip on her throat, cutting off her air. Buffy smiled as she slid the stake between the Kakchiquel's ribs, its glowing eyes going wide as it felt the penetration. Then it was dust.

The other, a copper-skinned bald man, got a handful of her hair and yanked. Buffy did not fight his strength, but used the momentum. As he hauled her backward and down, she bent farther and flipped into an aerial somersault. In his surprise, he let go, but not before his hold on her hair tugged painfully at her scalp and it began to bleed. He held strands of her hair in his hand as Buffy landed on the concrete floor behind him.

The bald vampire turned toward her, a bewildered expression on his face, and Buffy struck him twice in the face in quick succession, batted his arms out of the way, and then rammed the stake through his rib cage and into his heart. When he burst into a tiny whirlwind of cinder and ash, there was an audible pop, as though all the energy he had sucked from Camazotz had suddenly been released.

When she turned again, crouched in a battle stance, she saw Xander fire a bolt from the crossbow. It struck home and the leech was dusted. The other was nowhere in sight, and Buffy had to assume Xander had gotten them both.

The sounds of their combat seemed to resonate there in the basement, but they were like an echo now. Buffy sensed that it was almost over. Prepared to slay the remaining few vampires opposing them, she turned to see that Oz and Willow had cornered two Kakchiquels who cowered behind the corpulent, writhing form of Camazotz. The demon-god was chained to the floor and he alternated between a catlike mewling and a sinister snicker that made Buffy wonder if he was not quite so unhinged as she had imagined.

Oz leaped over the captive demon and upon one of the Kakchiquels, a huge claw slashing right through the bat-shaped brand on its face as the werewolf drove it to the ground.

Willow faced the other, lifting her hands, her clothes rustled by an invisible wind that often accompanied her sorcery these days.

Buffy began to relax and to think ahead to their next step, linking up with Lonergan and the others again in the continued search for Giles. She began to turn toward Xander to tell him to contact Lonergan on the headset he wore.

An alarm went off in her head, spurring her to glance quickly back at Willow. The final Kakchiquel feeder ran along beside Camazotz, probably hoping to use him as cover from the sorceress's magick. Willow seemed to carve the air with her fingers, beginning an incantation.

Buffy saw what was about to happen and cried out, but too late.

The vampire leaped over Camazotz's massive arm.

Willow cast her spell.

It missed the Kakchiquel and instead struck the huge, iron chain that bound Camazotz's right arm to the concrete floor. The heavy chain turned to ice and the demon-god uttered a wet, soul-searing laugh as the ice shattered. With one hand unleashed, the demon began to sit up, tearing at the chains, struggling to free himself.

"Damn it," Buffy muttered. "We *so* do not have time for this."

The Bronze was in ruins. Explosives had blown in the entire outer wall, scattering debris and concrete dust all over the floor and crushing one end of the stage. With the wall shattered, the sunlight had streamed in and incinerated seven or eight vampires quickly enough that Anna Kuei, the Slayer, had not been able to get an accurate head count. It was a comparatively small nest, but there were other Kakchiquels scattered throughout the building, in the kitchen and in storage and office areas.

Or there had been.

Now she crawled out from beneath the shabbily constructed stage and wiped blood from her eyes. When she glanced up, she saw Wesley moving across the floor with his old repeating crossbow in his hands. Other Council operatives moved about the wreckage, searching behind the bar and under toppled tables. Wesley spotted her and an expression of intense relief washed across his bearded features.

"Oh, Anna," Wesley said, hurrying toward her. "When I didn't see you out here . . ." His words trailed off as he focused on the cut across her forehead.

"You thought I was dead?"

He cast a sheepish glance at his feet. "I confess I feared the worst."

A shudder went through the young Slayer. *Does that mean you have no faith in me?* she thought, but she did not dare to ask aloud. Anna dreaded the answer. For all his sometimes amusing mannerisms, Wesley was a skilled combatant and a brilliant strategist with a knowledge of the supernatural that was nothing short of extraordinary. He was not merely *the* Watcher, but had briefly been Watcher to both the Lost Slayer, Buffy Summers, and to Faith, the Prodigal.

*Faith.* Just the thought of her caused a tumult of emotions to swirl in Anna's heart; warm memories, grim dignity, and despair. The older Slayer had never hidden her past. But when Sunnydale had fallen the Prodigal had returned to the fold and selflessly thrown herself into the effort against the Kakchiquels. Faith had been the bravest person Anna had ever met, and though she had teased him, it had always been obvious that Faith had respected Wesley Wyndam-Pryce.

"Anna?" Wesley prodded now, brow furrowed with concern. He touched at the cut on her forehead and she hissed. "Are you sure you're all right? Do you feel at all disoriented?"

"No," she said quickly. "Sorry. I'm all right. I just . . ." she gestured toward the stage. "I heard something moving in the dark beneath the stage. Once I was down under there, it was easy . . . well, their eyes gave them away. But there wasn't a lot of room and for a second I thought they had me."

Wesley did not smile or try to comfort her with platitudes. That was not his way. Instead, he gave an approving nod and clapped her on the shoulder. "But you're standing right here. Well done, Anna."

The young Slayer slid her stake into the leather sheath on her hip. The other operatives in their unit were still exploring every dark corner and shadow of the remains of the club and she picked her way toward the back to offer what help she could. It helped to turn her mind to things other than death and combat and evil.

For all her training, Anna had almost no experience in the field. The four vampires she had dusted in the past five minutes were more than she had ever previously seen in one place at one time, and here she found herself smack in the center of what some of the Council operatives had referred to as the biggest anti-vampire operation in centuries. Though she would never let Wesley see it in her, Anna was frightened.

But Faith had believed in her. Wesley believed in her.

And Anna Kuei was not going to let them down.

In the balcony that overlooked the main floor of the club, something rustled in the dark. A pair of operatives had already been up there, but Anna knew what she had heard. The hush of clothes moving, someone shifting in a hiding place, the belly of a snake across hard-packed desert.

Her body tensed, muscles coiling. Her gaze ticked toward the stairs and she slipped her stake out of its sheath again. Quiet descended upon the Bronze as the Watcher and the Council operatives noticed her stealthy movements.

"Anna?" Wesley said.

The Slayer went to the bottom of the stairs. She heard the sound again, some dark creature huddling beneath a table perhaps, clinging to the remaining shadows, the threat of the sun far too close.

"Come down," Anna said, her voice hard and cold, though her every nerve seemed to prickle with a combination of fear and exhilaration.

With a bang, a table up on the balcony seating area toppled over. A dark figure rose, whipped a dusty tablecloth around its shoulders, stepped onto a chair and then the balcony railing, and leaped out over the concrete debris-strewn floor of the Bronze.

The vampire, tablecloth over his head, landed in a crouch in the sunlight. Wesley fired a bolt from his repeater crossbow but it went wide. The target was in motion. A Council operative took a few shots at it with a pistol and the vampire grunted in pain as one of the bullets tore through its shoulder. But all the gunshot really did was add to the vampire's momentum as it careened across the rubble for the outside, trying desperately to get away from them.

Anna sprinted across the floor, leaped onto a table and then jumped up into a flying drop kick that cracked into the back of the runner's skull. The Kakchiquel was driven forward, lost his balance and sprawled through the huge opening that had been blown in the wall to land on the sidewalk in front of the Bronze.

In the sun.

The vampire tried to curl up under the tablecloth but one of his legs was already on fire. Groaning, the creature struggled to rise.

Anna tore the tablecloth from its head. The vampire

snarled, fangs bared in blind fear and rage, the sun gleaming off the perfect black of the bat-shaped brand around his eyes. He burst into flame, fire rushing all over his clothes, his hair roaring like an oil-soaked torch. The fire consumed him, and the vampire burst into a small explosion of cinder and ash, like confetti raining down on New Year's Eve.

For a moment she stared at the ash that fell, there in the sun, with the wind swirling it along the sidewalk, carrying the remains of the creature away. Anna shivered. This was her sole purpose, the slaying of vampires and other creatures of the night. But it was a hideous thing to see.

Footsteps crunched the rubble and she turned to see Wesley approaching. He had donned a communications headset.

"Yes, Ms. Haversham. We'll be right along," he was saying. Then he glanced up at her. "I think we're through here, Anna, don't you?"

The other operatives had begun to spread out to the buildings on either side of the Bronze. The mission parameters called for them to check adjunct buildings for any annexes to the main nest. But she had a feeling they'd taken care of the real trouble, so she nodded at Wesley.

"Ms. Haversham has informed me that the unit at the Hotel Pacifica has run into some difficulty. The rest of our squad is to continue on to their next objective, but the group at the Pacifica would appreciate our aid."

Anna's heart was still racing from the thrill and chaos and utter terror of what she had just been through. But she had to confess to herself that, in a way, she liked that feeling.

"Let's go," she said.

Together they climbed into one of the Humvees the unit had at its disposal. Its engine rumbled and the vehicle shook her so that she could feel its power in her bones. On the way to the industrial park north of town, Wesley updated her on communications that were coming over his headset. It seemed that of the five units deployed, two had already moved on to their second targets. Their own unit was soon to do the same. But there were two—one at the new high school, and the one at the Hotel Pacifica—that had encountered great resistance at their initial target locations.

Just words, until they pulled into the parking lot at the Pacifica. The property around the hotel was all lawn, with a broad parking lot in front. The structure itself had a Spanish influence like so many older buildings in the area, but this was a five-story stucco monstrosity painted a pastel tangerine. By all rights, it ought to have been abandoned ages ago, but according to Wesley, it had been in operation right up until the vampires had occupied Sunnydale. From Anna's perspective, it was the sort of place frequented by tourists who could not afford a place right on the ocean, two-bit sci-fi conventions, and real estate salesmen who snuck off for a few hours twice a week with their secretaries.

Not anymore.

Now the only guests at the hotel were vampires.

An enormous hole had been blown around its main entrance, a gray Humvee jammed half in and half out of that hole, its body a burned out husk, still smoking. Several of the white sunsuits the vampires wore during the day lay on the pavement, fluttering empty in the breeze, their owners dusted.

The unit of Council operatives was nowhere to be seen, save for a man and woman who stood behind a green troop carrier, shouting into their headsets.

Wesley drove toward them, and they looked up gratefully as the Humvee came to a lumbering stop nearby. Anna jumped out, Wesley only steps behind her, and ran to the pair. The woman was Terri Blum, but Anna did not recognize the man.

"What happened?" Anna asked quickly.

The man glanced at her and Terri turned to him. "The Slayer," she said.

"Thank God." He heaved a sigh of relief as he studied Anna and Wesley. "Here's our situation. The population of the nest was much higher than estimated and it looks like they were expecting us. They're spread out all through the hotel, but their numbers are much greater than ours. My unit is in there but we've already suffered at least three fatalities, possibly more."

All three of them stared at her. After a moment, Anna met Wesley's gaze. The last thing she wanted to do was go into that building; she did not even want to look at it. But in the back of her mind she envisioned the men and women who were searching the darkness within for vampires, imagined the glowing eyes of the two

Kakchiquels under the stage at the Bronze, and she knew she had to go.

"All right," she said. Then she spun and started for the front of the garishly painted hotel. After a moment, she glanced back at Wesley. "You coming?"

He smiled. "Wouldn't miss it."

# CHAPTER 2

Chains snapped, and Camazotz was free.

For a single moment, silence descended upon that dank basement, a quiet interrupted only by the rattling wheeze from the demon-god's throat and the drip of moisture from the pipes that ran along the ceiling of the basement. The tiny sound drew Duffy's attention and she glanced up at the pipes. Dozens, perhaps hundreds of small bats still hung from the metal shafts or clung there, wet charcoal bodies almost blending.

Buffy had almost forgotten the bats. While she and her friends had slain the vampires around Camazotz, the flying rodents had barely stirred. Now, though, they began to emit tiny squeaks, disturbed by the demon's motion and anger. Camazotz was, after all, the god of bats.

"You!" the demon thundered, his voice thick and grating.

Though it seemed impossible, Camazotz was not merely more obese than the last time she had seen him, the demon was simply bigger. The basement ceiling was perhaps fourteen feet and Camazotz fell short of striking his head on the pipes by no more than two. His head sagged forward on his shoulders, lips open in a kind of eternal slur, yellow drool sliding over the needle-like fangs in his mouth.

According to what Buffy had learned from Willow and the other Council operatives, the god of bats had made a terrible mistake when he had one of his Kakchiquels make Giles into a vampire. Camazotz had fed his vampire servants on his own blood and it had charged them with a horrible, demonic energy, enhanced them and made them deadlier than their brethren. But given what they had discovered in the basement, it now appeared that once Giles took control, Camazotz had been made into little more than a battery, a thing to be worshiped for the sake of the power he provided, a horrible dark communion of which all Kakchiquels shared.

There was no way to know how long ago Giles had locked Camazotz in this basement, but the shambling, rotting creature seemed a pitiful, lunatic caricature of his former self. The demon moved only a few steps from the spot where he had been chained. The last survivor of the vampires who had been feeding from him when they came into the basement slunk back into the shadows behind him, but Camazotz paid no attention to him. Nor did the demon appear to notice

Willow and Oz, who were only a few feet in front of him.

"Willow, Oz, get back." Buffy motioned for them to come to her and Willow complied immediately, backing away from the demon. The werewolf snarled low and sniffed as if taking Camazotz's measure by scent alone. Then Oz turned his snout away, the awful stench of the moldering flesh of the demon-god driving him back. The wolf trotted over behind Buffy and Willow, and a moment later, Xander joined them.

Camazotz moved slowly, almost staggering. His rheumy eyes glared down at them, but Buffy suspected he barely saw the others.

"You . . ." the demon-god said again, slobber spilling from his lips. "Slayer. Look what you have done to me. I came to these shores to retrieve my wife and your interference led to this. If not for you . . . Zotzilaha would not have had a host powerful enough to resist me. I might have torn her away and kept her with me . . . and punished her appropriately. But with your body as host . . . my only choice was to destroy her!"

Buffy stiffened, reached behind her and drew the sword from the scabbard across her back. "Blah, blah, blah . . . Willow already told me the whole sad story. How you killed your wife . . . twice! And that's somehow *my* fault?"

With her sword brandished before her, in a standoff with the hideous beast, Buffy laughed softly in disbelief.

"I don't think so."

Camazotz began to shriek in a high pitch that drove like nails into Buffy's eardrums, and the demon-god rose up to his full height and started to shake. As an answer to his shriek, the bats on the ceiling began to cry out in return. They fluttered down into the basement in a black cloud of rustling wings and sharp talons, swarming around Buffy and her friends, ripping at their faces and arms as they tried to defend themselves.

With her sword, Buffy rushed at Camazotz, whose eyes crackled with sorcerous energy. Buffy brought the blade around in a low arc that slashed a gaping wound across the demon-god's gut. Blood and noxious bile spilled out onto the floor.

Willow and Xander struggled with the bats, but Oz batted them away, ignored them, and joined the fray. Oz growled as he leaped up onto the god of bats and began to tear at his face. One of the pointed ears on the demon's head was ripped off as the werewolf dug deep furrows into the rotting monster's scalp.

Camazotz cried out in pain and hauled Oz off him, then tossed the werewolf across the room. Buffy swung the sword around her head again and was about to slash the blade down when Camazotz pointed at her and orange, fiery energy lanced across the few feet that separated them. It cut into Buffy and she shouted in pain, riveted in place. She began to shudder with the pain of it coursing through her.

With a roar of agony, she pushed toward him, feeling as though hurricane winds were buffeting her to keep her away. Still she went on. Arms heavy with the effort and exhausted from the bone-deep pain, she brought the blade up and cut off his clawed hand.

"There you go," she said through gritted teeth. "Another stump to go with those stubby little wings."

Camazotz only grunted.

Buffy drove the sword into him and began to cut upward. But even as she did so, she noticed that the first gash she had opened in his torso had begun to close.

"What does it take to kill you?" she yelled.

"Buffy!" Willow called. "Get back!"

The Slayer did not turn, but neither did she hesitate. Once upon a time, despite her love for her friend, she would have wanted to know Willow's plan. But she knew now that that was a mistake. She trusted Willow completely, and it had nothing to do with the authority and confidence in her voice.

Camazotz reached for the Slayer with his remaining hand, fingers crackling with power. Buffy dodged, then backed quickly away, sword held high in front of her.

Gunfire erupted nearby and a quartet of holes were punched into Camazotz's chest. *Xander,* Buffy thought. Across the basement, Oz growled low and dangerous and started toward the demon again.

"Oz, wait!" Willow commanded.

The werewolf froze at her order, yellow eyes on Camazotz.

When Buffy had moved back beside Willow, she

glanced at the sorceress and saw that she held Xander's crossbow in her hands. All around them on the floor were the charred or battered remains of bats. Some of them still squealed and dove at Xander, who was bleeding from multiple tiny wounds, but he easily knocked them away as he took aim at Camazotz again.

"I've got it, Xand," Willow said. "Camazotz is hard to kill, but he has a weakness. It took me a few years, but don't let anyone ever say I don't do my homework."

"What is it?" Buffy asked.

Willow smiled grimly. "Ever wonder why all those ancient civilizations made so many things out of gold?"

With that, she grimaced as though in pain, laid a finger on the bolt nocked in the crossbow, and whispered a spell in what sounded like French to Buffy. The crossbow bolt turned to gold.

"Alchemy," Willow explained as she raised the crossbow and took aim. "The secret is, it only works if you're not using it for personal gain."

Xander shot a bat and it spun away in bloody pieces. "Well, that sucks," he said. "Who made that rule?"

Camazotz screamed furiously and shambled toward them, entire body now crackling with demonic energy. Buffy raised the sword again, but she need not have worried. Willow fired the crossbow and the golden bolt pierced the demon-god's blistered hide in the middle of his chest.

Anna had dust in her eyes.

She did not allow herself to consider that it was the

remains of vampires, of walking corpses, as she brushed at her face and shook the ash out of her hair. The Hotel Pacifica had seemed deserted at first but the instant they entered the stairwell she and Wesley had been attacked by a pair of vampires. For a moment, as she drove one of them down on the stairs with stake in hand, and the other leaped upon her back and yanked at her spiked, pink hair, she had thought it was over for her. In her mind, she had already begun to apologize to the people she felt she would be letting down.

Then Wesley had fired a bolt from his repeating crossbow, and dusted the vamp on her back. A second later she rammed her stake through the heart of the one beneath her on the stairs, and it was done. Anna cursed herself for having allowed her mind to accept defeat so readily.

"Are you all right?" Wesley whispered, his gaze darting about, alert for any further sign of attack.

Anna nodded. She steeled herself and continued upward, with Wesley following close behind. The design of the building's interior was modern and at the second floor the landing opened to a wide, carpeted hall with contemporary art decorating the walls. The corridor was littered with the bodies of the dead.

"Dear God," Wesley whispered behind her.

As they passed the elevator, Anna paused. Voices, shouting from upstairs. The sounds of battle.

"Listen," she told Wesley.

He paused, put his ear to the elevator doors, then his eyes narrowed. "Top floor. Mission schematics indicated a ballroom up there."

Anna punched the Up button. Moments later there was a small ding and the doors slid open. They were both prepared for an attack from within but the elevator was empty. As they stepped in and Wesley pressed the button for the fifth floor, the noises from above grew louder.

"If they notice the elevator coming up?" she asked him.

Third floor.

Wesley slid his headset firmly into place, ready to relay their situation back to the unit commander outside, or to Ms. Haversham at their ops center. He did not answer her, but rather pressed his back against the wall of the elevator as it whirred upward, and lifted the repeating crossbow. Anna saw that there were only four bolts left in it.

Fourth floor.

Soft music poured from speakers above their heads.

Fifth floor.

With another pinging noise, the doors slid open on chaos. In a single glance, she took it all in: three more operatives dead or downed on the fancy carpet, probably twenty or more vampires under the faceted light from the chandelier, seven Council operatives cornered on the far side of the room, axes and crossbows and guns in their hands.

*Flamethrowers,* she thought. *Where are the . . .*

Then it hit her. One of the dead men downstairs had had an extinguished flamethrower on his back. In the epicenter of the ballroom lay the second of the men in this unit equipped with one, also dead.

"Wesley, the flamethrower," Anna whispered.

As she and Wesley stepped surreptitiously off the elevator, surviving operatives leaped at the vampires, axes falling, hacking. A crossbow bolt whistled into the cluster of vampires and one of them dusted. Someone threw a glass vial of holy water and it burned those it touched, but none severely enough to destroy them.

Anna studied the room quickly, and saw that the wall to her right had once been almost entirely glass. There were boards covering most of the wall now, but in the center was a glass door that had been painted black.

Anna rushed the nearest vampire from behind. Though she was far shorter than he was, she leaped up onto his back and wrapped her legs around him. With a fistful of his hair, she yanked his head back and he fell with her still riding him. He landed on top of her even as Anna reached around in front of him and thrust the stake through his chest.

He dusted, but she was on the floor.

They came at her then, five or six, she could not count. In the false glimmer of the chandelier above, their eyes flickered with unearthly energy. As one, they leered at her, fangs bared, the brands seared across their faces stealing away their individual identity and making them all the more hellishly terrifying for it.

Bracing herself on the ground, Anna swung her foot up into a kick that shattered teeth and sent one of them spitting blood. She tried to spin away from the others but they were on her, hands in her hair and all over her body. One of them slammed her face into the ground and she was dazed despite the carpet.

When she glanced up, she saw Wesley. He had the flamethrower and let loose with a stream of liquid fire as they ran at him. Two of them were set ablaze and ran screaming toward the stairs over near the elevator before bursting into twin puffs of smoke and embers.

As she attempted to shake herself free, she saw a Kakchiquel grab Wesley from behind and sink his teeth into her Watcher's throat. Blood spilled down Wesley's neck, staining his collar. His eyes were squeezed closed, but not the vampire's. The monster's blazing eyes were wide open and staring right at her.

"No," she whispered.

The silent killers turned her over. One of them, an Asian female who had been young when she was bitten, was a mirror image of Anna herself. Nothing had ever unnerved her quite so much as that.

"No!" she screamed.

With every ounce of energy in her, she swung her left hand up into a bone-crunching blow that shattered ribs in the vampire girl's chest and knocked her back. They were still all over her, but Anna was fearless now, with nothing left to lose. She twisted her legs, grabbed up another vamp in front of her in a scissors move and then toppled him into a third.

A massive Kakchiquel with a build and features that made her think of a troll grabbed her by the shoulders and tried to drive her back down. Anna shoved her hand into his mouth, the skin of her palm and fingers tearing on his fangs, and she yanked down hard, cracking his jaw.

Then somehow she was up and away from them, whirling and ready for them, and the Kakchiquels hesitated, giving her a wide berth. The operatives shouted for her, even as they hacked at their own attackers. Two crossbow bolts cut across the room but only one found its mark, and the odds were still against them. Only four operatives were left alive now, not including herself and . . .

"Wesley!"

Anna cried his name and turned to see him sagging in the arms of his attacker. His killer.

*No. Not his killer.* On the floor five feet away was the corpse of an operative, a shotgun clutched in his dead hands. She ran to the dead man, shot an elbow into the face of a vampire who tried to stop her, picked up the weapon and turned it toward the blacked-out glass door on the other side of the room.

Anna fired and the glass exploded and sunlight streamed in. Its reach was only enough to touch three of the vampires who stood near it, but that was enough for her in that moment. They shouted in agony and began to burn, then scuttled into the shaded parts of the room.

The light also fell on Wesley and the leech attached to him. The vampire grunted and then reluctantly let him fall to the ground, its face charring as it retreated.

Anna ran to her Watcher, crouched over him and felt for a pulse. He was still alive, but she did not know for how long.

Anna glanced around the room again. No one moved. For a moment it was a stalemate, though the Kakchiquels still outnumbered them four or five to one. At length, the troll-face whose jaw she had broken began to hum, low and guttural, like some ritual chant of ancient days, and all the others joined in. The demon magick in their eyes glowed brighter and a sinister calm fell over them; they began to close in.

The Slayer looked down at Wesley, so pale, eyes fluttering under his cracked glasses, and a stillness touched her own heart as well. She stood and faced the leeches, her only weapon herself. The anxiety and fear she had been battling all along dissipated and a certainty grew in her. Anna Kuei was the Slayer, and she was not going to let anyone else die here today.

"Come on, then. Try me."

Their chanting continued and Troll Face even laughed, eyes glowing with magick and menace.

Then the spark went out of his eyes. He grunted and blinked in surprise as the orange glow faded completely. Anna flinched, then looked quickly around to see that all of the Kakchiquels were reacting in shock as they felt the energy leave them, their eyes returning to normal.

The chant died.

Anna smiled. It seemed that whatever had given the Kakchiquels their enhanced strength was gone now.

"Well, this is interesting," she said, standing astride

Wesley. She glanced over at the four surviving Council operatives. The panic in their faces had been replaced by anger and a dark satisfaction. They hefted their weapons and began to move in. Crossbow bolts struck two of the vampires and they disintegrated.

The young Slayer moved toward the others, who had clustered together. The vampires stared at her. With the black tattoos across their eyes all she could think of was a pack of raccoons caught raiding trash cans.

"Don't let any of them leave," Anna told the operatives.

"No problem," one of them, Tom Canty, replied grimly.

The vampires broke and ran and the operatives went after them, Canty shouting into his headset commlink the news that the Kakchiquels had lost the additional power that gave them their edge. The tide had turned. Anna lifted Wesley, put him over her shoulder the way a fireman would have, and ran out after them. Amidst the carnage, she started down the stairs. As she reached the second floor, Anna felt him stir.

"What happened?" Wesley croaked weakly.

"I don't know. Whatever enhanced them, it's gone."

"Do you think we could stop for a Pepsi?" he asked.

Anna laughed as she walked down the stairs toward the first floor, shifting his weight on her shoulder. "I'm taking you to a hospital. I thought you were half dead."

"Certainly not," he protested. "And while I appreciate the concern, you can put me down now."

She set him down, but his legs were weak and he had to lean on her.

"Thanks to you, Anna, the ruffian did not have the

time to drain very much blood from me. Certainly not more than the Red Cross would have. But, you see, I always faint when I give blood. When I come around, I get a Pepsi and a cookie, and I feel much better."

With his arm slung around her, Anna navigated them both around the Humvee and the rubble that blocked the main exit and then they were outside in the sun. She cast him a dubious sidelong glance.

"You want a cookie?"

Wesley smiled, his eyes bright with amusement. "If it wouldn't be too much trouble."

Camazotz died.

With a single gasp of fetid breath, the god of bats rolled his eyes upward and fell back with an impact that shook the floor. A moment later, his flesh began to boil and run as though it had been doused in acid. Then his body collapsed into a pool of mucus, dark energy crackling in it, sizzling, and then dying out.

"Take your time, Willow," Xander muttered. "You couldn't have done that when we came in?"

"Well," the sorceress replied defensively. "He seemed pretty helpless until, okay, the bats."

"And the homicidal demon rage," Buffy added.

"And that," Willow agreed.

Something shifted in the shadows of the far corner, and only then did Buffy remember that there was still a Kakchiquel left alive. Its glittering eyes gave it away. It stared at them, the bat tattoo on its face gleaming black in the dimly lit room.

The vampire tried to slip along the far wall, moving toward the exit.

Oz had taken human form again, though there was still something feral about him. He approached the rest of the group, a dubious expression on his face. "Does he think we don't see him?"

"I've got him," Buffy replied. "We've wasted too much time already."

She started for him, putting her sword back into its scabbard and pulling out the stake. The vampire began to hiss. Then the filthy orange light flickering in his eyes simply died. Stunned, the vampire blinked several times, and glanced over at the exit again.

"You'll never make it," Xander told him.

Buffy saw in the undead thing's eyes that he knew he was trapped. To his credit, he did not try to run. Instead, he lunged at her. Even without the power leeched from Camazotz, he was fast; fast enough to get a grip on her throat before she staked him.

The ash showered down onto the floor, but Buffy had turned back to her friends before the last of it touched the concrete. Oz stood by Willow as though he were some innocent bystander, completely distanced from the savagery of moments before. His oversize tunic hung on him even larger than before, stretched out as it was, and he had his hands in his pockets as though he were bored. Xander had his sidearm out and was popping a fresh clip of ammunition into it.

As Buffy walked toward them, Willow watched her expectantly.

"You're quite the witch," Buffy told her.

A coy smile flickered across Willow's features. "That I am."

With Buffy in the lead, they headed out the door and into the stairwell. The stink from the remains of the demon-god was nauseating and did not go away as they started up and away from the basement. On the first floor, they stopped briefly and moved out into the main corridor. The alarms had stopped and the sprinklers had been shut off. A pair of Council operatives had been left behind as sentries in the fire-blasted main foyer. But they were alone. The rest of the floor had been cleared.

"I wonder if there's a way to set off all the sprinklers in the building at once," Buffy wondered aloud.

"We checked the schematics," Willow replied. "The system isn't set up that way."

"Giles has probably killed the water to the whole building by now anyway," Xander said. "Just in case."

Buffy nodded slowly. Of course Giles had shut the water main off. Or, more likely, had someone else do it. Though her stomach tightened uncomfortably every time she thought of him that way, she knew the monster was still as cunning as her Watcher had been in life. The first floor was clear. They had eliminated a lot of opposition already. But it would be foolish to think that they had the upper hand.

"Check in," she told Xander.

He tapped a button on the side of the headset he wore. "Lonergan, this is Harris. We've swept the basement, fourteen hostiles no longer our concern. One of them was Camazotz."

Buffy could not hear Lonergan's response, but Xander frowned deeply as he spoke.

"Will do," Xander said. "We'll rendezvous with you there." He glanced up at Buffy, Willow and Oz. "Let's go."

It was Xander's turn to lead now, as they headed back into the stairwell and started up at a steady jog.

"They're just hitting the fourth floor," Xander said. "A few stragglers dusted, no losses from our camp, but no sign of Giles or any large contingent of Kakchiquels. The mayor's office is empty. Lonergan's sixth sense is still picking up vampire presence up there, but now he's getting something else, a kind of static, to the south. We'll hook up with them on the fourth floor, complete the sweep, then investigate whatever's blocking him.

"Oh, and looks like the little power drain the vamps are experiencing now that Camazotz is dead is spreading. The last few they dusted had no light in their eyes, and word is coming in from some of the other units. The same thing's happening all over town."

Willow grinned. "Chain reaction. If they're all just ordinary vamps now, our job is practically done."

"No," Buffy said grimly. "Not yet."

They had passed the second floor landing and were halfway to the third when a low growl came from behind them. Buffy turned to see that Oz had begun to change again. This time, however, he did not change all the way. He was hunched over, his face still recognizable despite the fur covering it, his hands curled into claws.

"Oz, what is it?" Willow asked, her voice clipped and heavy with authority.

His words were a guttural snarl. "Caught a familiar scent. Wasn't sure what it was at first. Now I am."

"What is it?" Buffy asked.

Oz stared at her a moment. Then he sniffed the air again.

"It's Angel."

# CHAPTER 3

The Humvee rumbled through the streets of Sunnydale and Anna thought of all the times she had turned on the news and seen footage from urban war zones. With her hands tight on the wheel, she could not help but glance around as she drove. On the horizon, above the town, she saw three pillars of black smoke trailing up and away from locations where operatives were burning out vampire nests. She spotted a couple of demons packing some bags in an old Thunderbird, obviously clearing out of town before the Council took complete control. *A good sign*, Anna thought.

"You really have done quite well today," Wesley said happily, between cookies.

They had found a convenience store whose owner had remained in business by cooperating with the Kakchiquels. He had locked the door and hidden inside, but after a few minutes of knocking, he had reluctantly opened the door. The man had not asked a single question nor said a word to them and when Wesley had tried to pay for his Pepsi and a bag of Oreos, the man had waved them away.

"Just get them. Wipe the vermin out."

It had surprised Anna to hear those words. This man was what she would call a collaborator, but the more she thought about it the more she realized that he would have lost everything if he had closed his business down. And without people who were willing to cooperate with the vampires, those who were truly prisoners, living in fear, would have starved to death.

"We're working on it," Wesley had told the man.

Now he had the small bag of Oreos on the seat beside him and was munching away contentedly. As she took a turn past Hammersmith Park, Anna glanced at him.

"I was terrified," she confessed, her voice small.

"You'd never have known it," he said firmly. "Truly. You were magnificent. Faith would have been very proud."

A warm feeling rushed through Anna and she beamed. She was about to respond when Wesley held up a finger and bent forward slightly. A low buzz came from his headset, and Wesley nodded as he listened to whatever message was coming through.

"Yes, of course. Excellent. We're on our way," he said.

"On our way where?" she asked.

Wesley slid the headset down to rest around his neck and grinned at her. He still seemed a bit weak, but his color was coming back. Anna figured Oreos just sort of had a magick all their own.

"Our original unit has their second nest under control. Ms. Haversham has asked us to proceed to City Hall to aid with efforts there," her Watcher explained with great satisfaction. "So it appears we're needed after all."

In the pool of light spilling in from the shattered window at the end of a fourth-floor corridor, Father Christopher Lonergan stood as still as he was able and reached his mind out. He could feel that there were more of them, but while their dark intentions usually gave them away, he sensed only two or three individual vampires still in the building. In the courthouse, however, well, that was another story. It had taken him some few minutes to orient himself, but when he did he realized that there was a kind of psychic screen blocking him from sensing anything in the adjacent building. That was the source of the static he felt.

Giles was hiding, which meant that he *knew* Lonergan was with this unit. It seemed the king of the vampires had his own spies. The thought was chilling.

"Right, then," he called gruffly. "Nothing else up here. All of you with me now."

With Harris, Rosenberg, Osborne and the Slayer off on some quest of their own, Lonergan's unit was comprised of some fifteen operatives, ten men and five women. Minutes before, as the unit spread out to sweep the fourth floor, Harris had contacted him on the commlink again and announced that their little squadron would be delayed. Lonergan wanted more details, of course, but neither Harris nor Rosenberg was willing to provide any. They promised to be along just as soon as they were available. The priest did not like it. What was the point of having the Slayer along, not to mention a werewolf and a witch, if you could not take advantage of their abilities?

Now, alert to any possibility of attack, Lonergan led his unit down the stairs. He carried a metal crossbow with a pistol grip. He had modified the contemporary weapon so that it would fire wooden bolts, rather than trust the antique weapons that many other operatives and Watchers favored. He also wore a heavy two-headed battleax across his back in a leather case.

Then there were the guns. All of the men wore them, but Lonergan had not needed to use a side arm as yet. More useful was the flamethrower Hotchkiss wore on his back, its mouth sputtering as though in anticipation.

On the second floor, they spread out across the corridor, all eyes on Lonergan. He raised a hand and they all froze, waiting for another instruction. Though it was only a faint trace, he sensed a vampire not far away, along the corridor that led west. With nothing but static anywhere else, it was tempting to head in that direction, but reason dictated that such a weak presence could not be Giles.

Suddenly, the priest saw movement back the way they had come, two figures emerging from the open stairwell. Adrenaline surged through him as questions raced through his mind; how had the vampires gotten so close without him sensing them?

"Down!" he shouted as he raised his crossbow.

The operatives in the path of his shot dropped and rolled quickly, coming up again ready for a fight. Others who were not in the line of fire took aim with their weapons, some unholstering pistols, more than one leveling a shotgun.

Lonergan sighted along the length of the crossbow and his finger tightened on the trigger. Then he saw the face in his sights: Wesley Wyndam-Pryce. The Watcher held his hands up as though he were being robbed, his antique repeater crossbow aimed at the ceiling. Behind him stood the Slayer, Anna Kuei. A momentary expression of alarm traveled across her face and then was replaced by a relieved smile.

"Wesley," the priest said tiredly. "Next time, y'might want to give us a shout before you pop your head 'round the corner."

"Yes, well, we thought it best to be as quiet as possible. I was just about to try to contact you by commlink when we heard your lot moving around up here. Like a pack of elephants, really. So much for stealth."

The insult rankled Lonergan and he was about to snap off a nasty retort when he spotted the raw puncture wounds on the side of the Watcher's neck. His respect for Wesley ratcheted up a notch or two and he frowned and gazed at the man again.

"Ms. Haversham informed you of our current situation?" Lonergan asked.

Wesley nodded once.

"Right then, it's what we're here for, lads and lasses," Lonergan told them all. "Let's get to it."

Wesley was exhausted and weak but he would collapse and die there on the floor before he would let Lonergan see it. Even with Anna he had taken pains not to reveal just how debilitated he had been by the bite of the vampire. Now as the Council operatives all hurried down the eastern corridor, then turned right at a junction, it was all he could do to keep up.

But hate drove him on. His teeth were set together, jaws clenched, and he drew the back of his left hand across his mouth, beard scratching his skin. Rupert Giles had never seemed to really respect him, but though Wesley would never have admitted it to his face, the man had been a sort of hero to him. Once he had become accustomed to being Buffy's Watcher, Giles had never toed the line for the Council, never cowtowed the way the Directors so often seemed to demand. Wesley remembered wishing he himself had that sort of backbone.

Now there was nothing he desired more than to drive a stake through the heart of the thing that had infested Giles's body. While he suspected others might have difficulty separating the two, he had no trouble making the distinction.

Rupert Giles was dead.

This thing they called by his name was his murderer.

All morning he had hoped that fate would bring him to this very place, and so it had. But getting here had almost cost him his life. He felt faint, his throat dry, and he stumbled slightly as they ran through the breezeway above the street that separated City Hall from the courthouse.

"Wesley?" Anna asked, her strong grip on his arm supporting him.

"I'm all right," he said quickly, straightening up.

He checked the crossbow's chamber. He had nearly run out of bolts back at the Pacifica and had only found a handful more in the Humvee. But it would be enough, he was convinced. Now that he knew that whatever had given the Kakchiquels their demonic energy was gone, he had begun to believe in his heart that he could destroy Giles himself.

At the far end of the breezeway, the doors into the courthouse were propped wide open. Wesley dismissed the idea that they had been left that way by accident. It was either an invitation, or an indication that they were not considered a threat at all. A shudder went through him and he wondered when Willow and the others would rendezvous with them.

Lonergan stopped ahead and motioned for them to go upstairs. The breezeway had been their passage from one building to the next, but apparently the vampires were gathered above them.

On the third floor, Lonergan led them out into the corridor where a massive set of double doors marked the entrance to one of the building's courtrooms. There was a sense of menace all around them now, hanging in the air like the foreboding weight of the sky just before a thunderstorm. The way the operatives moved, their every glance, revealed that they all felt it as well.

The corridor was empty. The room beyond the doors was silent.

Lonergan motioned for Hotchkiss and Bianchi to move up in front of the door with their flamethrowers. Then Quinones stepped between them with his shotgun slung down at hip level. Lonergan gave the signal and Quinones blew a huge hole in the doors where knobs and locks had been a second before. Then Lonergan and another operative kicked the heavy doors open.

Hotchkiss and Bianchi were the first through the door, fire streaming in hungry arcs from their flamethrowers and igniting three . . . five . . . six vampires who rushed them as they entered. The leeches all roared their pain, but two of them actually continued to stagger forward, skin and clothes ablaze, before Quinones blew their heads off.

The courtroom was perhaps forty feet square, the high windows blacked out by heavy tapestries that hung over them. The lighting was dull and flat and gave a surreal, almost two-dimensional look to everything within. But the vicious beasts in that room, the dozens of vampires gathered there for a last stand, were all too real, all too three-dimensional. Though their eyes no longer flickered with the tainted blaze of ancient magick, they were a fearsome sight, the bats tattooed black across their contorted features, fangs bared, all hissing as one hideous, ravenous pack.

The melee began.

Wesley pushed into the room with the other operatives around him. He shot an elbow at a vampire, knocking it back at the cost of a sharp pain that spiked up his arm. Another appeared, leering, before him, and he fired a bolt at its chest and was bathed in a cloud of ash for his trouble. Around him, in his peripheral vision, he saw the battle raging on. The Council operatives kept together in a rough circle, backs to one another, letting the enemy come to them. Lonergan's crossbow was batted out of his hands and the barroom-brawler-turned-priest headbutted the vamp in front of him, then whipped the ax from behind his back, threw off its leather case, and swung it in a wide arc. The gleaming blade decapitated one Kakchiquel and sank into the shoulder of another.

A female vampire, almost completely naked save for a vividly colored serpent tattoo all across her body, lashed her hands toward Wesley. The long clawlike nails of one hand gashed his cheek and jaw, cutting the skin beneath his beard. The Watcher expertly fired another bolt and she was dusted.

Wesley glanced to his left and saw Bianchi driven down beneath a horde of bloodsuckers, and it pained him to know that there was nothing he could do for her. Quinones was there a second later, and he fired the shotgun into them. None of them were destroyed by it, but they scattered, wounded, leaving Bianchi's corpse behind. Wesley felt faint again, sweat dripping down his face, blood matting his beard. Ever since he entered the room he had been gazing around, hoping to see Giles.

At the back of the courtroom, the door that would lead into the judge's chambers opened. A lithe, dark-skinned vampire whose bat-brand was stark white emerged from the open door. Wesley recognized Jax from file descriptions. A moment later, Giles followed. Despite the absence of his glasses, he looked for all the world like the wry, benevolent man he had once been.

Giles spotted Wesley noticing him. One eyebrow raised, the vampire king gave him an ironic smile, and waved.

"So glad you could make it, Wesley!" Giles called across the shattered benches and the corpses and the blood, his voice somehow rising above it all, even the blast of a shotgun nearby.

Bitterness welled up inside Wesley. His gaze was torn away from Giles by another attacker, and he dusted it with the last bolt in his crossbow. He was now weaponless, exhausted, and vulnerable. But he would not give up. With a snarl of hatred he started across the courtroom. A vampire grabbed his shoulder and Wesley shook the thing off, turned and pummeled it with three quick blows that knocked the monster unconscious.

The Watcher wavered on his feet, but he refused to fall.

Then Anna was at his side. One of her arms had a long gash in it, but she seemed not to notice as she brandished her stake in front of her.

"Time for him to die," she said.

Wesley nodded, and together, they started for the dais where the judge would preside over the courtroom. The door to the chambers was behind it, and Jax still stood there.

But the vampire king had slipped away through the chaos of the battle.

Giles was gone.

Buffy could barely breathe. Once again the two souls within her swirled together, thoughts and emotions and memories mixing, making it almost impossible to separate one from the other. Buffy-at-nineteen knew that in her own time, Angel was still alive, fighting for his own redemption in Los Angeles. She had accepted that they could not be together, but her love for him was an ache in her heart that never quite went away. Buffy-at-twenty-four remembered that feeling distantly, but she also felt the long years of her imprisonment, during which she had wondered so many times if Angel would come for her; why he had not; what had become of him.

Together, upon Buffy's escape from El Suerte, the two spirits residing in her body had come to one conclusion: Angel was gone. The only thing that would have kept him from her was death. What little Willow had been able to tell her only seemed to confirm that. Angel had gone to face Giles, to free her, and had never returned.

In his love for her, a love that both of them had sacrificed for the greater good, Angel had risked his life and his chance at redemption. Now Buffy would discover what had become of him. With Xander and Willow alongside her, she followed Oz down a side corridor on the second floor of City Hall. Oz was a werewolf again, and he prowled the carpet, sniffing the air, following the scent he had picked up before.

Angel's scent. Which meant that somehow, Angel was alive.

"Hey," Willow said softly, her hand reaching out, her fingers entwining with Buffy's as they moved swiftly after Oz.

Buffy glanced at her, saw the concern in her friend's eyes.

"If it's him, and he's here . . . and he's still alive?" Willow said. "Gotta consider the possibility that he's evil."

"I know," Buffy said, offering Willow a sad, lopsided smile. She reached up and touched the hilt of the sword that was slung in its scabbard across her back. "I used this on him once before. I'll do it again if I have to."

"Or I could," Willow offered. "If you want."

"Let's see what's what first."

Willow nodded and they kept on after Oz. Xander had passed them by and now he and the werewolf stood in front of a door at the end of the corridor. Oz paced back and forth anxiously, sniffing at the door. Xander gazed at Buffy and Willow expectantly.

"Check this out," he said.

On the door was a red and white metal sign inscribed with the words NO ADMITTANCE. Buffy frowned as she studied it. It was the sort of thing you might see in the back of a restaurant; she recalled a similar sign on the door to the boiler room back in Sunnydale High. But it was awkward and out of place on the upper floors of the neatly appointed government building, and they had not seen anything else like it on other doors, save for the entrance into the basement.

Buffy stared at the sign, then glanced down at Oz. "Angel?"

The werewolf growled low and snapped at the air. The Slayer took that as a yes. She tensed, and was about to kick the door down when Willow called out for her to stop. Buffy looked at her curiously. The sorceress waved her hand in front of the door with a flourish.

*"Munimentum prodeo!"* she commanded.

With those words, a breeze whirled around them from out of nowhere. A static hiss filled the air and the door was suddenly blocked by a shimmering barrier of crackling energy the dark purple of a painful bruise. The smell of sulfur was in the air.

"Boy, whoever hung that sign wasn't kidding," Xander said in a hushed tone.

Willow gazed at Buffy. "Defensive spells. Not just a ward against entry, but a powerful destructive magick. If you'd touched it, I'm guessing we'd be scraping Slayer off the walls. Not to mention the blood on our clothes? You know those stains never come out."

The dark energy of the barrier crackled from floor to ceiling in front of the door. Buffy glanced at it and then back at Willow.

"Well, good thing you caught it. Y'know, 'cause of the dry cleaning bills and everything," Buffy said, a thin smile on her face as she stared at her friend in wonder. "How'd you know?"

Willow shrugged. "Just sort of sensed it, I guess."

"Oz didn't," Xander noted, gesturing to the werewolf,

who had retreated a few paces down the hall. "And he's got wolf-nose. Pretty cool, Will."

"Can you get us through it?" Buffy asked.

The sorceress stared thoughtfully at the sparking current of magick that barred their way. After a few moments, she closed her eyes and whispered.

*"Perfringo contego."*

Willow opened her eyes and twisted her mouth into a grimace. Several minutes passed and she merely stared at the door. Twice, her fingers moved and she began to draw symbols on the air, but then stopped and shook her head.

"I can't just shatter it," she said. "And I've tried to come up with a spell that would protect us enough that we could just pass through, but as adept as I've become in certain areas of magick, that's just not something I can do."

Disappointed as she was, Buffy did not fault Willow. If not for her, they would never have even known the barrier was there, and Buffy herself might actually be dead. Still, she was not simply going to stand out here in the hall.

"We could come back," Xander suggested. "The rest of the unit may need our help."

"Lonergan would have contacted us," Willow replied, still staring at the door. "That's what the commlink is for. Your headset is still working, isn't it?"

Xander tapped it, then nodded. "As far as I can tell."

Buffy drew her sword again and took a few steps down the hall. "How long do you think it would take me to get through the wall?"

Willow stared at the sword. "Oh. Wait. A thought is here!" She walked to Buffy and gazed down at the engraved blade. "This thing is already enchanted somewhat, and that might help. But maybe I could put a spell on the sword, a protective ward like the one on the door."

"I get it," Xander said. When he narrowed his eyes in thought, the crescent scar on his face crinkled and seemed almost to shine. "The thing blocking the door is like electricity. If you introduce a separate field of similar energy to it, you might short it out."

Willow grinned.

Oz padded up to them, gazed at each of them in turn, and then went back to his spot just down the hall. He sniffed the air and Buffy realized he was keeping watch for them.

"So what are my chances of exploding when I do this?" she asked Willow.

"Minimal."

Buffy held the sword out in both hands. "Do it."

Willow nodded intently and studied the blade. She placed both hands above it, her fingers perhaps half an inch from the metal, and began to sway slightly as she muttered words in a guttural, ancient-sounding language that Buffy thought might be German or something older. She was never more aware of her own linguistic limitations than when she was around Willow.

A light seemed to glow around Willow's face as she spoke, and then that weird illumination traveled down along her arms and to her fingertips, and finally to the sword. A kind of aura surrounded the blade, tinted green. It sparkled with power, as did the barrier in front of the door, but this spell seemed somehow smoother, calmer.

The hilt of the sword vibrated in Buffy's hand and the skin of her arm prickled. She glanced around at her friends.

"Back up."

They did so immediately, moving away to stand with Oz. Buffy held the sword with both hands and hacked at the magickal barrier. As the blade slashed through the field of crackling energy, a sound like a buzzsaw ripped the air. Light flashed green and black as night, and then the barrier dispersed. The metal NO ADMITTANCE sign fell off and hit the floor. Behind it was a small, simple placard with the words TOWN PLANNING BOARD.

In the corridor, all was still. Buffy reached out, touched the knob, and found that it was not locked. She pushed the door open. The windows inside had been bricked over, but light spilled into the room from the hall. The planning board's office was a shambles, with massive file cabinets tumbled over and papers spilled across the floor. A desk had been turned on its side; a computer monitor lay shattered on the ground.

There was another light in the room as well. A dark, unearthly glow, the same bruise-purple as the barrier in front of the door had been. It emanated from a spot off to the left, out of sight of the doorway.

Buffy stepped inside and the others followed her. On the left side of the room, in the midst of more destruction, she saw Angel.

"Oh God," she whispered.

Angel hung suspended in a sphere of dark magickal energy, his arms straight out from his sides, legs dangling beneath him, as though he had been crucified. He was dressed all in black, his jacket torn and hanging loosely, a long gash across his cheek. But it was his position that stunned her the most, for he hung there just as he had in her dream, when he had advised her on dealing with Giles. There were differences, of course.

A stake protruded from his chest, perfectly positioned to have destroyed his heart.

Yet somehow he lived.

# CHAPTER 4

"Angel?" Buffy whispered.

Oz appeared beside her and in a heartbeat he transformed from wolf to man, face contorting, fur withdrawing, as if it were the simplest thing in the world.

"Is it really him?" she asked, staring at her former lover where he hung encased in a shimmering sphere of sorcerous power.

"His scent? No doubt," Oz confirmed. He scratched a bit at his unruly hair. "Really him? Couldn't say."

The vampire's eyes were closed and he looked peaceful, as though he were lying in a casket at a funeral home. The thought came to Buffy unbidden and she pushed it away. Though she wanted to deny it, she felt certain it really was him. The line of his jaw, the strength in his sculpted features.

"Willow?" she asked. "This is the same as the spell out there?"

"I think so, Buffy, but . . ." her words trailed off.

Buffy turned to find all three of them looking not at Angel, but at her. Willow's chest rose and fell unevenly, as though she were overwhelmed with emotion. Oz raised one eyebrow. Xander glanced down and shifted on his feet, then looked back up at Buffy.

"What?" she demanded.

"Not to make a big deal out of it, Buff, but . . . did you notice the stake?" Xander asked.

Buffy sighed and looked to Willow. "It missed. I mean, it had to have missed, right? He's still here."

"Now there's some logic," she replied supportively.

Oz cleared his throat. "And blood. There's some blood, too."

Buffy stared at him. "So?"

"He's been gone five years," Xander said. He rested his crossbow on his shoulder, his expression grim. This was the soldier in him, she knew, the man he had become. "If he's been here all that time . . . I don't know. I just think you should be careful, is all."

"Careful as I can be," Buffy said. She held the sword up to Willow again. "Spell me."

But even as Willow lifted her fingers above the blade and began to chant, Buffy heard the soft rasp of a voice behind her, speaking her name. With a start, she let the sword drop down, the fingers of her right hand aching with the grip she had on it. And she turned.

Angel's eyes were open. A wan smile spread slowly across his features.

"Found you," he rasped, the words laden with static as they passed through the sphere that was his prison.

"Actually, we sorta found you," Xander corrected.

"Semantics," Oz added.

Buffy barely heard them. Willow touched her arm, whispered to her that she should stay away from the sphere, but she could not help herself. Carefully, eyes locked on Angel's, Buffy moved closer. She could feel her hair beginning to stand up with the static energy that emanated from the dark sphere.

"Angel."

Her heart felt cold in her chest and for a few moments she forgot to breathe. No matter how deeply she loved him, she had known those years ago that they were not destined to be together. It seemed fate had other things in store for them. But now . . . he had been a prisoner all this time, just as she had. He had come to find her, to save her, and now it seemed it would be up to her to save him.

"I dreamed I heard your voice," he croaked, smile broadening. "Guess it wasn't a dream."

"Hang on, Angel. We're getting you out." Buffy turned and raised the sword up in front of Willow again.

Crucified, hanging there in perfectly preserved agony, Angel uttered a small, soft laugh. "I wish you could," he said. "But, Buffy, you can't."

She faltered. More than anything, she wanted to argue with him, to tell him that they had broken the magickal barrier protecting this place and they could free him from that same magick. But in her heart she knew that wasn't what Angel was talking about.

Slowly, her throat dry, a chill running all through her, she turned to face him again. "The stake?"

Angel's smile was gone. Some of the light was gone from his eyes. "I came to find you. I don't know how long ago it was. Time does weird things in here. I confronted him . . . Giles. We fought. That's why the place is such a mess. Sorry I couldn't pick up."

He laughed softly, but his expression was still grim.

"He beat *you?*" Xander asked.

"Hardly," Angel replied bluntly, frowning. "I cleaned his clock. But he had this spell all set up. Like a magickal bear trap, and I walked right into it. I was trying to escape as it closed in around me, and he caught me with my guard down."

With a tilt of his head, unable to move his arms, Angel motioned toward the stake.

"Even though he isn't really Giles, he has all of Giles's memories and personality, his grudges. He remembers when I tortured him and he wanted to return the favor. Time is sort of frozen around me. If you try to free me, I'm dead."

Buffy shook her head slowly, fighting back the tears that threatened at the corners of her eyes. The two souls within her were completely unified in their sorrow, in grief. It would have been better, she—they—thought at that moment, if she had never found Angel at all. Then she could have imagined he still lived, somewhere. But this was almost more than she could bear.

"There has to be a way," she said, her voice tight.

"Maybe we can find a way to take the stake out before breaking the spell that's holding you."

"Buffy," Angel said, his voice low and hard now. "Look at me."

She did. What she saw in his eyes made her want to turn away, but she would not do that to him. Not now.

"The damage is done," Angel told her.

Willow came to her then and Buffy hugged her friend close, taking comfort in the familiar feel of her arms, the smell of her hair, the simple caring in her eyes. The Slayer still held her sword, but its tip hung toward the ground, dangling from her hand.

"There's got to be something we can do, Will," Buffy said. "When is it enough? Giles. My mom. Your parents. Anya. Faith. When do we get to the point where we've lost enough?"

Buffy looked past Willow to Xander and Oz. Xander's steely exterior had given way completely now, and she could see that he shared her pain. Oz, though, was not looking at her at all. He looked so deceptively normal, so human, but his brows were knitted and he sniffed at the air. Then his eyes widened.

"Guys?" Oz said.

As one, Buffy and Willow spun toward the door.

Giles stood leaning casually against the wall just inside the room. The moment was completely surreal. He wore soft black shoes, gray pants and a blue cotton sweater that seemed amiably rumpled. As she stared at him, taken aback by his sudden arrival, she almost expected him to be holding a book, or a cup of tea. He seemed startled by the sudden attention directed at him.

"Hmm?" he mumbled absentmindedly, as though he'd been caught not paying attention. Then he straightened up, slipped one hand into his pocket, and scratched idly at the back of his head as if in contemplation.

"Right. Sorry. Just lost in the spectacle. As to the point where you've lost enough? I don't think any of you have reached it yet, really. Not when you consider that you're still alive. I'll guarantee you this, though. I'm working to remedy that even as we speak."

The illusion shattered, along with Buffy's heart. This was the second time she had faced him like this, heard his voice and *known* that the evil she had dedicated herself to combatting had tainted him, reached out and claimed him . . . and just as it had the first time, several nights earlier, it crushed her. And yet it hardened her as well.

"It's over for you," Buffy said, sword at the ready. "Your little kingdom is done."

"Tsk," he said. "No 'Giles, old boy, so good to see you? I've missed you so?' Nothing?"

"You're not Giles."

"Oh, but I am, Buffy," the vampire king said, his tone making the words sound as though he found them delicious. "I always underestimated the process, you see. My soul is gone, certainly. But whether you like it or not, I *am* Giles. If I weren't, if I didn't love you like my own daughter, would you still be alive? Would you have gotten this far? I saved your life, Buffy, I helped you get out of Sunnydale, but only because I knew you would come back. They called Faith 'the Prodigal,' you know. The Council did. But you are the real Prodigal, aren't you? You've come back to me."

The Slayer began to shake her head, revulsion flooding through her, fingers flexing on the hilt of the sword. The vampire king's eyes locked on the blade.

"You know that, though, don't you? Otherwise you would not have accepted my gift. You would not have brought it with you. Did Angel recognize it, I wonder? The very sword with which you killed him, and sent him to Hell. The weapon with which one of us, my dear girl, my own daughter, might very well soon kill the other."

"I'm going to tell you one last time," Buffy snarled. "I'm not your daughter. I brought this just to give it back to you. Blade first."

"As you once did with the knife Faith used to try to kill you," Giles replied.

Buffy blinked, hesitated.

"Surprised?" the vampire king asked. "You shouldn't be. Deny all you want, but I *am* Giles. I made you what you are. You could not kill Faith, and you won't be able to kill me when the moment arrives. I want you to join me, Buffy. Be what you were meant to be. Together we will be unstoppable."

With a shake of her head, Buffy stood a bit taller, held the sword higher. "See, that proves it right there. Giles was never that stupid, or that arrogant."

"Actually, I always thought he was pretty conceited," Xander put in.

Giles glared at him. "I'm amazed you're still alive, boy."

In response, Xander fired a bolt from his crossbow. Giles sidestepped easily and it *thunked* into the wall behind him. With a low, menacing growl, Oz transformed again, and Buffy wondered how much strain it caused him, how much control he had to have to shift back and forth like that. The werewolf stalked forward, lips curled back from its snoutful of gleaming fangs.

Behind them, Angel's voice came weakly through the sphere around him. "Be careful," he said. "Remember what he's accomplished. Don't underestimate him."

"We never have," Willow said, her tone guarded. She lifted her hands and a soft green light began to dance among her fingers.

"Nor have I underestimated you, sorceress," the vampire king said, scandalized. "But I know Buffy. This is too personal for her. She's likely already staked a claim on my head, I'll wager."

Buffy hesitated again. He was right, of course. But if that was what he expected, maybe the best thing to do was surprise him.

"You know what, guys?" she said to them. "Nobody likes a know-it-all. Whoever kills him gets ice cream later."

For the first time since they had discovered him lurking in the room, Giles seemed off-balance. She was glad.

"Dammit!" Xander muttered.

His face was alive with conflicting emotions and he held one hand to the headset against his ear, listening. When he raised his eyes and looked at her, Buffy knew that there was trouble.

"Lonergan," Xander told her. "They need backup or they're dead."

Her gaze ticked toward Giles. He wore a broad, Cheshire-cat grin, and Buffy knew then that this was precisely what he had expected. Even orchestrated.

"They're in the courthouse," Xander added. "Wesley and Anna are already there, but they're seriously outnumbered."

Buffy did not take her eyes off Giles. "Go," she said.

"Buffy, no!" Willow protested.

Oz snarled and began to creep closer to the vampire king, who silently beckoned for the werewolf like a back alley bully, urging him forward.

"Don't take him alone," Angel advised, his voice like some dim, buzzing echo in the room, a radio someone forgot to turn off.

"Go," Buffy repeated calmly. "Camazotz is dead. Sunnydale's pest problem is over. Help Lonergan finish the job on this nest. I'll be all right."

She did not look at any of them again, for she feared that she would see doubt in their eyes; doubt that she could or would kill this thing wearing the corpse of her mentor, her Watcher, her friend. Buffy strode forward, on edge, ready to defend herself, and faced Giles down.

"Out of the way."

"But of course," he agreed happily, and he stepped aside, moving to the other side of the room, away from Angel.

Xander and Oz went quickly into the hall, but Willow lingered, staring back in at Buffy. The Slayer nodded at her, expressionless. After a moment, Willow nodded back. Then she, Oz, and Xander took off down the hall, and Buffy prayed they would be in time to save Lonergan and the others.

And then she was alone with Giles, save for Angel, who could only look on, crucified, imprisoned, and eternally an eyeblink away from death.

Sunshine streamed into the courtroom from a single, tall, shattered window. Dust motes danced on the rays of light and the splash of day into the room was a beacon of safety. In the midst of the melee, as humans and vampires clashed, the undead leeches dodged around that splash of sun time and again. Even if they were backed up toward it, they seemed to feel the burn of it as they got close and managed to slip away.

Anna slid beneath a vampire's attack as though she were a reed bending in the breeze, her right hand whipped up and the stake sank into the vampire's chest with a satisfying thump. Even as he turned to dust, scattering all around her feet, she shot a low kick at another and shattered his knee.

Behind her, Wesley shouted, rage in his voice. "Dammit, no!"

Alarmed, she spun and was just in time to see Jax, one of his eyes blown out and gore streaked across the ivory tattoo on his face, pull an ax out of Lonergan's chest. Lonergan was dead, staring blindly up at his murderer.

The fight had hardened Anna. The death and the blood and the constant motion of her own bludgeoning fists and pummeling kicks had become a sort of song that rose up in her and swept her away from the grief she knew she should have felt at the loss of people who had been at least her comrades, and some her friends.

But with Father Lonergan's murder, she could not postpone mourning. Sorrow flooded her heart and hot, salty tears sprang to her eyes. Almost immediately, though, her anger surged forth. Only a few of her tears fell before the cold fury in her heart dried them.

The Kakchiquels knew she was the Slayer, and so Anna and Wesley were culled away from the other four operatives who still fought. Hotchkiss and Fuchs were across the room with two others Anna did not know. They were in a rough circle, still fighting, probably still alive because of the flamethrower Fuchs had appropriated from somebody's corpse. Liquid fire blazed out like dragon's breath and the vampires knew enough to keep back. One of the vampires had a gun, but only got off a single wild shot before Fuchs torched him. Then the four operatives began to work their way toward the pool of sunlight spilling through the high, shattered window.

Wesley swore again and Anna glanced at him. He had a shotgun that had changed hands twice in the past minute, from operative to vampire and now to Wesley. He blew the throat out of a Kakchiquel in front of him, severing its neck. It collapsed in a tumble of ashes even as the Watcher swung the stock of the shotgun back into the face of another vampire behind him.

Anna took a right hook from a pretty boy vamp with blond hair and bright blue eyes. The punch cost her a fraction of a second and in that time the vampire got his hands around her throat. Furious at this lapse on her part, Anna reached up, grabbed his hair and rammed his head down even as she shot her knee up into his face.

The vampire went down and she was on top of him, stake in hand. He dusted and Anna rolled away instantly, then leaped back to her feet. She found herself side by side with Wesley, a new wave of vampires moving toward them. When she shot another look at the surviving operatives, Fuchs was a corpse, trampled underfoot by vampires going after the other three. But Hotchkiss and the others had reached the sunlight, making them more difficult targets.

Jax capered a bit, prancing merrily with the ax over his shoulder, as he came to join the other vampires who were slowly surrounding Wesley and Anna. With his bloodstained, razor grin and the bone white brand tattooed across his ebony features, Jax was a terrifying, nightmare creature, scarecrow-thin and yet with the grace of a dancer. The Slayer tensed, determined not to let the lives of Lonergan and the others have been lost for nothing.

"Wait for them," Wesley whispered next to her. "Dust Jax quick as you can. It'll unsettle the others."

She nodded, though her newfound confidence was fading. There were a lot of them. Probably too many.

Jax stopped, cocked his head to one side and smiled, the gaping black hole where his eye should have been making Anna shudder.

"Finish them," Jax said happily.

As the Kakchiquels started forward a sudden snarl made them waver. In that instant, Oz was upon them. Hope surged within Anna as the werewolf attacked them, tearing the arm off of one of the vampires before driving another down beneath his primal rage and slashing claws.

"Wesley!"

The young Slayer and her Watcher glanced over to see Willow and Xander come running into the court-room. Jax and the other vampires turned as well, and Wesley took that moment to attack. With a triumphant roar that thundered from his chest he lunged forward and cracked the butt of the shotgun across Jax's face. The ravaged vampire crashed into the first bench in the courtroom and fell over, dropping the ax with a clatter. It slid under the benches. Kakchiquels tried to help him, and Anna knew that was her cue. She staked one from behind, kicked another out of the way and grabbed a third by the arm, keeping them away from Wesley.

The Watcher looked wild with his beard and his

cracked glasses and his face red from exertion. He shoved the barrel of the shotgun down and pressed it against Jax's throat, and he pulled the trigger.

It clicked on an empty chamber.

Jax grinned, grabbed the shotgun by the barrel, and pulled Wesley down on top of him. Anna tried to scream but no sound would come out. Her eyes were wide and she felt suddenly weak as she grabbed at the back of Wesley's shirt and tried to tug him away from the hideous circus nightmare holding on to him.

With one hand on either side of his head, Jax broke Wesley's neck. The crack echoed through the room. Anna opened her mouth, horror exploding in her like fireworks, but still she could not scream. Distracted, she was not fast enough to stop the three vampires that grabbed hold of her and threw her back against the judge's dais. Jax approached her, licking his lips.

"I've heard such rumors about the blood of a Slayer," he said. "Well, more than rumors, really. I only wish I'd been among those who got to feast on Faith's blood."

At last, Anna screamed. She bucked one of the Kakchiquels away and tried to rush Jax with her stake, but he knocked it from her hand.

They had her.

Willow's heart sank as she and Xander entered the courtroom. So many dead, only a handful left alive. Easily two dozen vampires still in the room, and Oz had dragged three of them away into a corner, where they sparred with him as though playing. But it was not playing. Willow feared for him, but she knew how hard it would be to kill him, and so she pushed that fear away. Oz would destroy them.

But there were more. Maybe too many.

She saw Anna and Wesley across the room, but not Lonergan. With effort she put a wall up between herself and her grief, and she acted. There were three operatives to her right in a pool of sunshine streaming through a shattered window, but eight or nine vampires surrounded them, darting in and out, searing their hands as they tried to reach the trio. Apparently their only remaining weapon was a flamethrower one of them had acquired, and between that and the sunlight, they were barely keeping the vampires at bay.

Willow raced at them. Two of the vampires sensed her or saw her in their peripheral vision, for they turned to her with their fangs bared, hissing. Silently, her whole body aching from the magick she had already performed that day, she cast a long-practiced spell and both of them burst into flames. Another tried to grapple with her, and she turned it to ice even as they fought. When she tore her hands away, it shattered.

Beside her, Xander fired a bolt from his crossbow and one of the Kakchiquels menacing the three surviving operatives turned to dust. He and Willow moved in.

Then Anna screamed.

The cry of anguish echoing in her ears, Willow spun to see what had happened. Jax and the other vampires had the young Slayer trapped, and Wesley . . .

"Wesley's dead," Xander whispered, his voice hollow. Then he shot a quick glance at Willow. "Save them."

With that, he sprinted down the aisle.

"Xander, wait!" Willow shouted. "I can—"

But she could not, for before she could finish formulating the thought, a powerful hand closed on her ponytail from behind and yanked hard. Willow staggered backward, yelping in pain. It was a female vampire, a woman with red hair cut into a rough shag, and piercings all over her face. She pulled hard enough that Willow lost her footing and her head slammed against the wooden floor.

For a moment, everything went black.

Her eyes flickered open and felt the woman's ragged cut hair brush her face as the vampire went for her throat. In that eyeblink, Willow panicked. All thoughts of magick went out of her; she could not remember how to do spells that would destroy this vile thing. Pinpricks of pain on her neck, and Willow closed her eyes again.

"Go away!" she screamed, every ounce of despair collected over the past five years spilling out of her in those three syllables.

The weight was gone from her. The feel of the hair against her cheek. The prick of fangs on her throat. All gone.

Willow opened her eyes and looked around. The vampire woman with the piercings was simply *gone,* but the others who had been clustered around the three surviving operatives were now staring at Willow in abject horror, their fanged mouths hanging open. They looked ridiculous, these terrified monsters, and they began to back away from her.

Willow felt blood trickling from her nose and her legs were shaky. She wasn't sure exactly what she had done, but it had cost her.

She glanced up, saw Oz lunging at the back of a vampire who was fleeing from him; saw Xander pick up a battleax from the floor. The young Slayer with her shock of pink hair and her pretty ceramic doll features screamed as Jax raked talons across her cheek.

Xander was quick and silent as he swung the ax sidelong at Jax's neck with all his might. The vampire's head was cut off in one stroke, and it bounced once on the floor before both head and torso dusted.

Enraged, the other four vampires who had attacked Anna now turned on Xander. Willow shouted in alarm but it was too late. They piled on him, punching and kicking and clawing and Willow saw Xander's arms flail as he tried to beat them away.

Willow ran for him.

Anna rushed at them, tore one of the vampires away. Her eyes went wide when she saw what was under him, what had become of Xander. Willow faltered, her heart seizing in her chest, ice running through her whole body as she saw the look on the Slayer's face.

"No," she whispered.

"The windows!" Anna shouted as she grappled with a Kakchiquel. "There are too many of them. We've got to take out the windows!"

All Willow wanted to do was curl up into herself. The

vampires who had attacked Xander were rising now, done with him. *Done with him.* She could not see him, this man who had once been a boy, once been her best friend, once stolen her Barbie dolls. Once kissed her, no matter the cost.

He was too still.

And Anna was right. Oz was cornered, tearing into one after another, but still there were fifteen, perhaps twenty. And only she, Anna, Oz, and the three operatives remained.

*Xander. Oh God, Xander.* He had saved Anna's life, taken vengeance for Wesley, and now they might all die anyway.

"No." She spoke the word not in simple denial, but with power. The blood began to flow more freely from her nose now and she felt faint, as though she might fall at any moment. Then a breeze blew up around her, the wind borne upon the magick she now called down to her. Willow held out her hands, closed her eyes and tilted back her head.

It frightened her to call upon the power of the old ones, the elder gods as they were sometimes called, the lords of chaos, because they never gave without a price. It might be paid today, or years in the future. But Willow thought she had paid enough already this day, and so with all the mystic strength within her, she reached out.

"The highest walls, the thickest walls, the strongest walls, like a flood they pass," she chanted, teeth gritted, barely aware of the tears that slipped down her cheeks. "No door can shut them out, no bolt can turn them back.

Like a gale wind they blow amid the places between the places. The sons of Eng, be with me now!"

Her voice rose with each word and as she spoke the power within her increased. Willow gathered it up, and then in one instant, she pushed it away, pushed it out of her. In her mind's eye she saw the room around her, saw the windows with their heavy tapestries, and she *pushed* at them.

She *pushed*.

And the windows shattered, and the tapestries burned and fell, and the sun streamed in the high windows, and the vampires burned and died, and the wind swept in, caught their dust up in eddies and swirls.

It was done.

The courtroom was a shambles, corpses scattered all over the room. The sun seemed almost blasphemous, the warm breeze so sweet and clean and so very wrong. That something like this should happen under the light of a perfect day, while the world rolled on . . . Willow Rosenberg believed in magick and she wielded it with power that surprised even her. But in that moment, she did not believe in plain everyday *magic* anymore.

Slowly, she walked across the room to where Xander's body lay. The other operatives started for her, but Willow ignored them. She heard Hotchkiss talking on the commlink, reporting in to Haversham or someone, but the words sounded foreign to her. Willow glanced at Anna, who knelt by Wesley's corpse and tried to adjust his broken glasses on the bridge of his nose.

"Oh no," Willow whispered, as she stared down at the

broken, savaged form of her friend. "What did they do to you, Xand?"

A thousand images flashed through her mind. She did not remember life without Xander, and the ache inside her when she realized she would now have to go on without him was infinite. He had always been her cavalry, her hand to hold. No more.

Oz, human now, laid a hand on Willow's shoulder. She froze, reached up to grasp his fingers, then let him take her in his arms. A sob escaped her, but only one. Only one.

"He was right, you know," she whispered. "The earth never opens up and swallows you when you want it to."

# CHAPTER 5

Angel writhed in torment as hellish as any he had ever known. Trapped within the smothering sphere of magick that yet preserved his life, he struggled. He had spent years in that terrible prison and yet he had survived worse in the past. What made this far more horrible was the stake in his chest, the knowledge that there would be no escape from this torture, for the moment the spell was shattered, he was ash. More than once, more than a thousand times in that five-year span, he had wished for the end to simply come and be done with. His death was inevitable now.

But he had never desired his own death as much as he did in that moment.

In the room that had been his prison, Buffy held the long sword out in front of her, the runes engraved on it dark with age. He knew that sword all too well, for once she had been forced to impale him upon it. Now Angel only wished she could do it again. Much as he tried, he could barely move, not even to lower his arms. He hung there like a scarecrow as he had done for so long, the wooden shaft already in his heart.

In all that time, he had never expected to see Buffy again. Now he stared at her, amazed by the woman she had become, and saddened at the same time. Here was a warrior. Her blond hair was tied back carelessly, her body chiseled with muscle, tight as a whip. Her face was different now, the cheekbones and jaw more defined. Somehow, though, this was the girl who had always been inside her, the woman she was destined to become. This warrior had always been in her eyes, waiting to arrive.

But that had not been the totality of her, for there had been passion and love in her as well. Always, it had been there, and it had made him love her, made her the extraordinary Slayer, the amazing girl that she was.

And now Angel wished that he could crush that spark in her, because he feared that in this moment, it was either that, or Buffy was going to die. All because she still felt love for him.

"Buffy, whatever he says, don't listen!" Angel called to her, though he knew his voice would only come across dimly on the other side of his magickal cell, just as he heard their voices as a distant buzz.

*Their voices.*

Buffy's voice, and the voice of Rupert Giles. Or at least the monster he had become. Even now Giles glanced at him, an expression on his face that mimicked the intellectual curiosity he had so often shown when he was alive. But there was amusement in that expression now, a cruel humor that made a mockery of the man he had been. Just as the way he chose to dress so carefully mimicked who Giles had been as a Watcher. Certainly it was not an accident; the monster knew that the more he increased the illusion of benevolence, the more it would throw his enemies off-balance.

"By all means, Buffy," Giles said, his voice hushed and placating. "Do as Angel says. Don't listen to me."

The vampire king, so human in his soft cotton sweater, so normal looking, so Giles, strolled toward Angel and stared up at him for a long moment. Buffy could have attacked him then, might have reached him with the sword even before he could turn, but she didn't. She hesitated.

"Kill him!" Angel yelled.

"You could," Giles agreed, not even bothering to look at her. "Or you could join me, as I've asked. You can feel the rightness of it, Buffy. I know you can."

Buffy took a step forward, sword rising. "You're pretty cocky for a guy who's about to be kitty litter."

Giles smiled, chuckling softly. "You haven't changed a bit."

It was so familiar, and Angel could see it working on Buffy even as the alarm bells went off in his own head. She had to see what he was doing, preying on her feelings for him, her memories. She had to know it.

But it was working.

"Buffy!" Angel shouted again.

Finally, Giles turned to her, his back to Angel, who could only watch and listen.

"Give yourself to me," Giles said smoothly, intimately. "It's the right thing, Buffy. Become the daughter we both always wanted you to be, and I promise that after, I'll let Angel go."

Buffy's sword wavered. "You'll just let him go? What about the stake, moron?"

"I did this to him. Do you really suppose I cannot undo it? You know me better than that. Of course, after you're with me, you might change your mind about releasing Angel, but a promise is a promise. I'll let him go even if you don't want me to anymore."

As Angel watched in horror, Buffy lowered her gaze, gnawing on her lower lip, considering the offer.

"No!" he screamed. "Buffy, don't! He can't save me now! He's lying. The second I'm free, I'm dead. The only thing you can do for me now is to kill him!"

Giles spun, enraged, his features contorting as he fought to keep the face of the beast, the true countenance of the vampire, from showing. That would shatter the illusion.

"Oh, *do* shut up!" the vampire king snarled.

Behind him, Buffy raised her sword again.

Angel rejoiced.

Buffy mourned.

It tore her up inside to stand there and look at the two men who had meant more to her than almost anyone else in the world, and to know that both of them were dead. Her grief welled up from a place so deep within her that it was like some newly discovered heart.

Both of the souls within her, the spirits of Buffy-at-nineteen and Buffy-at-twenty-four that were twined together inside her, reached back in time for a memory, the moment that had led to this.

In the harbor master's office. Camazotz held Giles in his grasp, his life in the balance. The demon-god had instructed her to surrender herself . . . just as Giles did now. Camazotz had wanted her to sacrifice her own life to save Giles's and Buffy had known that the monster was lying, that if she gave herself up Giles was dead, that his only chance lay in her survival and the hope that Camazotz would keep him alive to use as bait for her later.

So Buffy had run away, crashed through a window and fled the scene, vowing to return to save him, to wrest him from the clutches of the god of bats. But her mind had been clouded by ominous warnings received from the ghost of Lucy Hanover, whispers Lucy had heard from an entity called The Prophet about a mistake Buffy would make that would have horrifying consequences.

The Prophet had promised to give Buffy a vision of those consequences, and instead had stolen her body, thrust her into this horrible future. For in truth The Prophet had been Zotzilaha, bride to Camazotz, herself fleeing from him. Now both Camazotz and his bride were dead, and so were so many others.

So was Angel, if not in this tick of the clock then in the next. And so was Giles. Somehow Buffy had to separate the two souls within her, her younger self returning to the past, traveling back far enough to prevent this future from ever occurring.

But in order to do that, she had to fall back once more on the first rule of slaying: she had to stay alive. No matter the cost, no matter how it broke her heart, she had to remind herself that this creature in front of her was little more than a demon wearing the mask of affection.

Still, Giles's words had their effect, his gentle, laughing eyes so familiar. The blade wavered in her hand. All was silent around her save for her own breathing and the crackle of magick that kept Angel both imprisoned and alive. And then Angel shouted at her again and she knew he was right.

Giles rounded on him, his voice a bludgeon. "Oh, *do* shut up!"

Buffy felt that voice cut into her and whatever illusion the vampire king had been able to maintain, shattered. He stood only a few feet away, his back to her. Angel hung in the air beyond him in a sphere of bruised light, and her former lover's eyes glowed as Buffy raised the sword and lunged at Giles.

Her arms brought the blade back, its edge whistled as it cut the air.

Giles moved so quickly that she could not counter. He dropped down beneath the arc of her attack and the sword passed above his head, even as he kicked out at her. His foot caught her in the gut, cracked one of her lower ribs, and sent her staggering backward. Buffy nearly fell over, stumbling several paces, and just regained her balance in time to avoid the vampire's follow-up attack. She dodged that blow and brought the sword up again.

He wasn't Giles anymore. His brow was swollen and ridged, his eyes feral, his lips bared to reveal fangs. This was the vampire, then, the mask now disappeared, all pretense gone.

"And I had such high hopes for you," Giles said sadly.

"Happy to disappoint you," Buffy replied.

She pushed away her hatred and anger and grief and focused only on him, on combat, on surviving. Angel exhorted her to action from within his sorcerous prison but Buffy no longer heard the words. All she knew was the tension, the moment between her and the fiend who stood in front of her, the heartbeat before they would clash again.

"Come then," Giles snarled. "If you must die, do it quickly. I've had enough of your interruptions."

Buffy smiled, enjoying his pique. "It burns your butt, doesn't it? You really thought I would give up, give myself over to you? See, in the end, that proves there's no Giles left in you. That's evil thinking, vampire thinking. Maybe you have his cunning, but you don't have his brains."

Her words had shaken him, and Buffy darted forward, slashing the blade down and severing his left hand.

The vampire screamed.

"Moron." She launched a high kick that connected with his chin and rocked him back.

He staggered, clutching at the raw, red stump at his left wrist. Buffy rushed in, her hands tight on the sword. She grunted with the effort as she swung the blade again.

Fangs bared, eyes gleaming yellow in the dim light, Giles leaped at her, disrupting her attack. He slammed his forehead against hers, their skulls clacking together, and then he rammed his knee into her gut and tore the sword from her grasp.

"Buffy, no!" Angel called, his voice so far away.

The vampire king raised the sword in his one hand and brandished it with the skill of the expert fencer Giles had been in life. Buffy backed up, glanced quickly around the overturned desks and cabinets of the room for some weapon, something with which to defend herself.

"You know," Giles said calmly. "I actually think I feel sad to have to kill you. Odd, don't you think?"

He attacked, sword slashing down at her. Buffy leaped back, then ran to her left. She dove over a desk and he pursued her swiftly, confidently. Buffy's heart thundered in her chest but now her emotions were truly clear. There was only necessity now.

*Don't die.* That was the rule. Survival was all that mattered, whether her younger self ever managed to erase this nightmarish era or not, there was nothing she could do for Angel or for Giles, only for herself and for all those who had suffered under the vampire king's predations.

The sword slashed down and carved a huge chunk out of a wooden cabinet as she ran past. Buffy ignored Giles and ran to Angel.

She stood staring up at him, this good, decent being who had waged such a long war within his own heart. Angel seemed alarmed at first but he must have seen something in her eyes, for he smiled.

"I've always loved you," he said, so quietly that she had to read the words from his lips.

Her entire body was tensed, her senses attuned so that she could practically feel the shift of the air in the room, could hear the swish of the fabric of the vampire king's clothes as he swung the sword straight down. Five years this creature had kept Buffy prisoner, during which she had worked her body every single day. She was faster than he remembered. The blade cleaved the air, falling toward her head.

Buffy moved.

The sword crashed through the sparking energy field that surrounded Angel and the sorcerous electricity surged up the blade as though it were a lightning rod. Giles jittered as the spell he had cast lashed out at him with enough dark power to kill a man.

But this beast was not a man.

With a pop, the sphere collapsed and faded as though it had never been. In that same moment, freed for the first time in years, Angel reached for Buffy.

Her eyes met his and she went to grasp his hand.

Their fingers never touched. Angel disintegrated in a blast of cinder and ash and the stake dropped toward the ground.

Buffy caught it as it fell, that carved shaft of wood with which the vampire king had killed Angel. Giles was stunned by the effect of his own magick but as she turned on him, raising the stake, he tried to block with the sword. She kicked his arm aside, though his fingers were still closed on the hilt, and she moved in close.

His features changed, and once again she was looking into the face of her former Watcher.

"Buffy," he said softly. "Please—"

"This is my mess," she whispered. "Time to clean it up."

Then she staked him, looking into his eyes. The dust of his remains sprinkled on her clothes as it fell to the ground, and Buffy fell with it, going down on her knees, there among the ruins of a fight that had begun years earlier and only ended now. In truth, though, she knew when it had all started.

Just as she knew that it was not over yet.

"Buffy?"

The gentle voice belonged to Willow. The Slayer let the stake slip from her hand to clatter to the floor and she turned to gaze up into the face of this valiant woman, this sorceress who seemed to have less and less of the girl she had once been in her features.

Oz was behind her. Xander was not. As she studied Willow's tear-streaked face, Buffy understood why.

And at last she cried.

Willow came to her and knelt by her and they held one another. Oz stood just inside the door, his eyes rimmed with red, his feelings for once plain to see.

After a time, Buffy stroked the back of Willow's head and whispered to her. "I have to fix this. I have to make this go away and you have to help me. I don't know what it will mean for you, but—"

Willow shushed her and nodded and promised that she would help.

Buffy held her close. "I have to make it right."

# CHAPTER 6

It rained all morning the day Xander was buried. The sky hung too low, a sagging gray canopy of clouds that seemed almost close enough to touch. It threatened at any moment to collapse and smother the earth in damp despair. But it was a hollow threat; there was no cataclysm, only the rain.

Only the rain.

Buffy and Willow stood together as the priest spoke at the graveside. Neither woman had an umbrella. The rain soaked their hair and clothes and Buffy felt her shoes sinking slightly into the sodden ground. She did not mind, nor did she even try to brush the wet hair from her face. Though it washed all the color from the world, cast everyone and everything in shades of gray, Buffy knew the color would return. More than that, she believed that this rain would begin to wash away the taint that Giles and Camazotz and the Kakchiquels had left on Sunnydale.

It might take a year of rainstorms, but it was a start.

The priest was Father Luis Vargas, a chaplain in the U.S. military. There were no clergy remaining in Sunnydale, though they were certain to return. In the meantime, however, now that the Council had done all the difficult work for them, the federal government had instituted a clandestine operation to restore the town, offering financial assistance to merchants and homeowners who had been driven out and wanted to return, or to people wishing to relocate there.

No mention of vampires was ever made.

Gangs, they said. Sunnydale had been the unfortunate victim of long-term gang warfare that terrified the citizenry, devastated the town's economy, and forced out many of its residents. This gang war had apparently also had a detrimental effect on surrounding communities, including El Suerte. Now, they said, thanks to a "police action," the gangs had been broken up, their leaders arrested, and a military presence was being maintained to prevent looting while locals and feds alike worked to restore the town to a functioning level.

Soldiers in the streets accepted the thanks of those who had lived in terror, as well as those who had cooperated with the vampires. But they were government soldiers, not Council operatives. After all they had lost, all they had sacrificed, the Council would not even be able to accept the gratitude of those they had liberated.

Buffy stared at the wooden casket and a tear slipped down her cheek. It was lost in the rain.

"It isn't fair," she whispered to Willow. "All he gave, and no one will ever know. His parents haven't even come back to Sunnydale. They should know what he did. That in spite of them, he was so brave and good."

Willow nodded, wiping away her own tears. "*We* know. I guess that has to be enough."

The priest droned on and it seemed to take forever, though Buffy was sure he was hurrying. And why not? He was a clergyman, yes, but he was just doing a job. This wasn't his town and they weren't his flock. The only reason Father Vargas presided over the service was so that the government could keep the cleanup as inconspicuous as possible. A brief memorial had been held the night before for all those who had fallen in the climactic battle in Sunnydale, their remains returned to their own homes for burial. Ms. Haversham had read the list of names and her voice had caught with emotion as she came to Father Christopher Lonergan, and then again when she read the name Wesley Wyndam Pryce.

Giles and Angel were on that list as well. The reading of their names was the only memorial either of them would ever have, for their names and the memories of their deeds were all that remained of them. Wesley and Lonergan would be returned to their families and given a proper burial, but for Angel and Giles, there were no bodies to inter.

The priest raised his hand and made the sign of the cross over Xander's casket. Buffy gazed at the rain beading up and streaming down the wood and tried not to imagine Xander looking back up at her. To the right of the priest, Ms. Haversham stood with a handful of Council representatives, all of them in black umbrellas and mourning clothes. On Buffy's left, just past Willow, Oz held an umbrella over Anna Kuei's head as if he could protect the girl from not merely the rain, but the world.

Buffy studied Anna and her heart ached for the young Slayer. She remembered what it had been like for her at that age, when she had first discovered her destiny. Anna had seen her Watcher die. Buffy had witnessed the murder of her own first Watcher, Merrick, and now Giles was dead as well. That wasn't how it was supposed to be. Slayers had such a short life expectancy; it was the Watchers who were meant to be left behind to grieve. If it were possible to be trained for such a loss, they were.

As Buffy watched her, Anna glanced up and their eyes met. Though the girl did not smile or even nod, Buffy felt a kind of understanding pass between them and a kinship grew there.

"He'd hate that," Willow whispered.

Buffy glanced at her. "What?"

Willow gestured toward the granite headstone that the Council had rushed into the ground. It was engraved with the years of his birth and death, and with his full name: Alexander LaVelle Harris.

"Alexander," she whispered. "He'd hate that."

Then Buffy understood. "Nobody ever called him that."

"Not in his whole life," Willow said, her voice hitching with emotion. "Except for teachers the first day of school. It's just wrong. It's all just . . ." Her hands fluttered up toward her face as though she did not know what to do with them and then she pushed wet strands of hair away from her forehead.

"*Wrong,*" Buffy echoed.

She stared grimly at the priest, who had completed the service and now turned to walk away. Ms. Haversham crossed toward Anna, spoke softly to the girl and then led her away, the young Slayer's shock of pink hair the one splash of real color on this gray day. Oz gazed for a long moment at the casket and then strode over to slip one arm through Willow's, a gallant gentleman escort.

"Hey," he said, greeting them both with that one word and eyes that had always communicated most of what he felt.

"Hey," Willow said softly.

He stared into her eyes then, perfectly still. "I was thinking it's like all along we've been in this huge house built out of our lives and everything we've been through up till now, and all of a sudden we stepped outside and the door shut behind us and we can't get back in."

A shudder passed through Buffy and she hugged herself, only now feeling the chill of the rain that soaked her clothes and skin. She wondered if she had ever heard Oz put so many words together at one time. He was usually so reserved. When he did speak, though, it was usually to make some wry observation, or to offer comfort. In some ways, his words now accomplished both.

Willow's face crinkled up and she wiped at her tears again and shook her head, her free hand touching her chest above her heart. "But I want to go back in."

"We can't," Oz said. His eyebrows rose and he tilted his head slightly, studying them. "Way I've got it figured, that door's locked now. But the thing is? There's the whole rest of the world."

Then this odd, sweet man who Buffy had known for years but never really *known* turned to her and one corner of his mouth twitched in what might have been a smile.

"At the end? He started to be Xander again, like he'd forgotten how to be and then someone reminded him. For what it's worth, I think that was you."

Her grief welled up within her then and Buffy found herself unable to respond to that. She offered a pained, wan smile, and then slipped her arm through Willow's on the other side and the three of them walked together away from Xander's grave.

"We're going to change it all," Buffy said as they left the cemetery.

"I think I've found a way," Willow replied.

Oz uttered a curious grunt. "I wonder if we'll feel anything."

Three days later, Willow sat at a broad oak desk surrounded by stacks of books and reams of notes in her own scrawl. Though the early morning sun streamed in the row of windows behind her, the green banker's lamp on the desk was still on from the night before. She had not slept.

Nearly a week had passed since the reclamation of Sunnydale and the extermination of the vampires who had inhabited City Hall. A search of the premises had turned up three entire rooms on the third floor of City Hall that were lined with books. Giles's library. He had learned what magick he knew from these ancient volumes and Willow knew that if she was going to figure out how to separate the two souls within Buffy, it would be here.

She set up camp that same night in the first of the rooms. Oz and Buffy took turns bringing her meals, most of which she did not eat. In the wee hours of the morning on which Xander was buried, she thought she found the beginnings of the answer.

Three days later, she was certain of it.

Exhausted, terrified by the thought of looking at herself in the mirror after days of little food and less sleep, she nevertheless felt a rush of excitement. She slid two books off the desk, both of which had pages that were yellowed and flimsy with age.

The previous morning she had allowed herself an hour to shower in what had once been the mayor's private bath and to change clothes, and now her hair was pulled up with just a rubber band. As she walked out of the room, she took the rubber band from her hair and shook it out, no longer needing to keep it out of her face. It felt good. *She* felt good.

It was shortly after seven in the morning when Willow rapped on Buffy's door. She paused briefly before knocking again. The third time around she heard Buffy moving inside and a moment later the door opened. There were several books on the floor next to a lamp but otherwise the room was spartan, a simple bedroll and a small duffel jammed with clothes all that Buffy had to her name.

Buffy wore a baby blue tank top and pajama pants and she stretched as she ushered Willow inside.

"Sorry to wake you," Willow said.

"S'okay," Buffy replied. "I was up late, training with Anna. She's actually pretty good." Even as she spoke, however, the Slayer's eyes went to the books in Willow's hands and then their eyes met.

"This is it?"

Willow nodded. "I had it sort of figured out days ago, but it took me a long time to figure out what to do with that knowledge."

Both women hesitated. After a moment, Buffy shrugged.

"What've you got?"

Willow walked over and set her books on the desk and then leaned against it. "A lot of this you know, some of it maybe you've only guessed. Some of it, honestly, I'm kinda guessing, too, based on what you've told me. The rest I put together based on research.

"Camazotz and Zotzilaha were Mayan deities, lords of the underworld, that sort of thing. Sometimes scholars mixed them up, which was sort of easy to do because they were pretty much a couple. Husband and wife, though obviously not *married* in that sense. He was the god of bats and both were more than demons, ancient beings who existed at the beginning of time but who gained strength from human worship.

"The destruction of Mayan civilization weakened both of them badly. For ages they couldn't even manifest on this plane. Zotzilaha was content with that but Camazotz needed worshipers. Somehow, in the late forties or early fifties by our count, he managed to open a portal to our world and came through. Zotzilaha did not want to come but he coerced her.

"She was miserable here. Hated every minute of it. Eventually she hated *him,* so much so that one night she attacked him and savagely mutilated his wings. Camazotz killed her physical form but her spirit escaped him before he could destroy that as well. As a ghost, if a deity can ever really be a ghost, she ran away, looking for a host body strong enough that she could elude or even destroy Camazotz.

"The demons had of course heard of the Slayer. So the ghost of Zotzilaha set out to find you. She masqueraded as The Prophet and used Lucy Hanover to help get to you, to warn you that you were going to make a mistake with horrible consequences. When Camazotz took Giles, you got desperate and she promised to show you the result of your mistake. All of that was pretty much accurate, but Zotzilaha only did it to get you to open up to her, to let her into your mind so she could force your spirit out."

Willow took a breath. The room was stuffy and the lack of sleep was beginning to get to her. She wished for a glass of water. The blacked-out windows were a harsh reminder of the evil presence that had inhabited this building and she did not like it.

As Buffy watched her expectantly, Willow cast a spell that restored the windows, eliminating the paint on them. It took the paint off the frame, too, but she thought that was a small price to pay for sunlight.

"Pretty much the way I figured it. How can you be sure about the recent stuff, though?" Buffy asked. She gestured toward the books. "You didn't get their lovers' quarrels out of books from the nineteenth century."

Willow smiled. "Vampy Giles was evil, but he still had some of Giles's old habits. He got it all from Camazotz, and he wrote it down."

A sad smile passed across Buffy's face. After a moment, she walked to the window and looked out at the street below.

"Here's what I don't get. The Prophet, whatever her name is, Z-woman . . . she was right. Her prophecy was true. Okay, instead of just showing me this future, she fast-forwarded my spirit five years. But to do that, she had to really be able to *see* this. The future, I mean."

"Exactly," Willow agreed.

Buffy turned to her, shaking her head. "No. You're not supposed to say 'exactly.' 'Exactly' is bad. You're supposed to explain it."

"You just did. Zotzilaha had precognitive powers, Buffy. She saw the future, saw what was to come, and she showed you, just as she said she would. But at that same moment, she used a spell of transference to move your spirit to the place your mind saw. When you first told me about it, I didn't understand how it could be done. What I was missing was how simple it really was. If she could show you the world through the eyes of your future self, she could cast the spell that would transfer you here. In some ways, it's like astral projection, only instead of you willingly leaving your body to wander the spirit realms, she used magick to force you out."

"Then she had to know," Buffy replied. "It was confusing at first when I, the two of me . . . whatever . . . when we both occupied this body for the first few days. But we adjusted 'cause even though there are two souls in this body, I'm still just me. When The Prophet pushed me into the future, she had to have sensed that the older me was really me. That she was no longer using my body as a host by this time. Didn't she know that she'd be destroyed?"

Willow could only shrug. "You know how arrogant those deities can be. I'm guessing she touched your future mind and soul, but just figured that the reason you were yourself in the future was because she had moved on to another host or returned to her own dimension by then. By now, I mean. It probably never even occurred to her that the reason the future you was still you was because Camazotz had killed her."

Buffy crossed her arms, muscles taut as she stared at Willow. Somehow she managed to look formidable even in pajama pants.

"Can you get me back?"

"I think I can undo the spell," Willow confirmed. Her pride and pleasure at being able to help made her smile and knock her feet against the desk on which she sat. "Actually, that's not the hard part."

Warily, Buffy raised an eyebrow. "What is?"

"Once I break the spell, the two souls in you will separate. You . . . the you who's supposed to be here, will stay here. The younger *you* will be pulled back automatically and return to its rightful body five years in the past when Zotzilaha, posing at The Prophet, came to you in our dorm room. But we both remember *when* that happened."

Buffy slumped against the wall again. "The night before I was captured," she said solemnly. "Giles was already dead by then, which means you've got to find a way to get me back earlier, to stop him from ever dying."

"Ex-act-ly," Willow said again, growing excited. "And I think I've figured out how. We just need to know *when.* Whatever mistake you made, you need to go back to that time and either stop yourself from making it or prevent the consequences from happening. We talked about that night at the harbor master's office when Giles was taken and you . . ."

Her words trailed off and Willow glanced away. She had been so thrilled by her discoveries, exhilarated by the sudden realization that she might actually be able to *do* this, that she had nattered on without taking Buffy's feelings into consideration. The last thing the Slayer needed was to be reminded that she had left her Watcher to die, and that because of that, thousands of others had been killed as well.

But Buffy surprised Willow by finishing her sentence.

"I ran," the Slayer said.

"Well . . . , 'ran' might not be, y'know, completely—"

"Okay. I threw myself through a window and killed a bunch of vampires and nearly drowned trying to get away."

Willow flushed.

"But I've been thinking about it, Will," Buffy added. "And I don't think that was it. I think I made my mistake earlier than that."

The early morning sun had warmed the room and it felt good, but still, goose bumps rose on Willow's skin. She waited for Buffy to elaborate, but the Slayer only smiled and walked toward her, picked up the books Willow had brought in, and gazed down at them.

"I'm not sure I ever really understood how lucky I was to have people who loved me for who I am, who were part of my regular Buffy-life and completely dedicated to taking part in my Slayer-life too," she said.

After a moment she glanced up and Willow saw that her smile had turned sad. Buffy proffered the books to her and Willow took them.

"Being the Slayer, the power that gives me, everybody calls it a gift. Way I'm seeing it, most every Slayer who ever lived had this burden dumped on them that they weren't prepared for. They fought the forces of darkness for a few lonely years, pretty much on their own except for their Watchers, and then they died.

"But me? I had you guys. And I never realized *that* was my gift."

Willow grinned sheepishly and suddenly all the sadness was gone from Buffy's face, just as magick had swept away the black paint that had kept the sun out of the room. In that moment, standing there in her tank top and pajama pants, and despite the time that had passed, Buffy looked once more like the new girl at Sunnydale High who had been so kind to her all those years ago.

"So what do we do now?" Buffy asked. "Do you want to talk to the Council or something before we do this?"

"Not thinking they'd believe us," Willow said. "And, okay, assuming they did? Not exactly sure they'd be the cheering section for what we have in mind."

Buffy frowned, shaking her head. Willow studied the Slayer's eyes, wondering if she could somehow see *both* Buffys in there.

"Which part of 'let's never have the army of vampires and avoid the mass murder' don't you think they'll like?"

"It isn't that," Willow said. "It's just . . . from their perspective, they won. What if, by going back, you don't prevent all this? What if you make it worse? And, okay, on a selfish, individual level, some of them might be thinking if you change the past, their present might be different in ways that are . . . unpleasant."

Buffy shook her head. "What could be worse than this?"

"Dying. That is, if you change the past, maybe some of us won't still be alive now."

"I never thought of that," Buffy said. "So what do we do?"

"Well," Willow ventured. "We could take a survey of the entire population of the world, find out if they mind if you tinker with the past to stop Sunnydale's little vampire holocaust. Or, y'know, we could just keep it to ourselves."

"I vote for Plan B."

Willow hugged her books to her chest. "I thought you might. Meet me in my office in an hour."

Shortly after eight-thirty, Buffy strode down the third floor corridor in City Hall. Already it was abuzz with the activities of Council operatives and government employees, both military and civilian, as they attempted to both restore order to Sunnydale and to cover up the circumstances that made their actions necessary. Only one or two people acknowledged Buffy as she passed, but that was all right. She recognized almost no one.

After a shower she had pulled on jeans, boots, and a green silk shirt that was almost too demure for her. It did not really seem to matter much. It had occurred to her that she ought to go and say good-bye to Oz and Anna, but then she had realized that there was no need. Within her were two spirits, and the Buffy whose soul belonged here would not be going anywhere at all. If she failed to alter the past, nothing here would change. And if she succeeded, no one would ever know.

She came to the door of the office Willow had

claimed as her own and knocked only once. Inside, much of the clutter in the room had been cleared, books stacked off to the sides now. White candles flickered, and they seemed oddly out of place in the sunlit room. A breeze blew in from the open windows and the candle flames sputtered but did not go out. Buffy had a feeling they would not go out, even in a hurricane.

Willow wore the same, rumpled clothes but did not look as tired now, despite her lack of sleep. She had been busy in that single hour, and the desk that had been piled with research was now barren save for two small metal dishes with incense burning in them, a small bundle of sticks and twigs tied with a red ribbon, and— lying across the wooden desktop—the same engraved sword she had used in her final combat with Giles.

"Am I late?" Buffy asked.

"You can't be late," Willow replied with a lopsided grin. "It's your party."

"You shouldn't have."

For a long moment they just looked at each other. Then Willow stood up from the chair and reached for the sword. She lifted it and beckoned for Buffy to approach.

"I have to cut you."

Buffy raised an eyebrow, taken aback. "Not that I don't believe you, but . . . why?"

Willow rested the blade point down on the wooden floor. "Souls are a sort of energy. All kinds of energy leaves traces behind. Souls make a mark on the universe, if you want to look at it that way. If you could see time, the energy of every soul living would leave a trail.

Zotzilaha put a curse on you that advanced your soul along the Buffy soul groove . . . and that sounds cool, but you know what I mean."

Buffy smiled. "I'm with you."

"The trick is, once I break the curse, you can't follow that same groove back or you won't be able to change anything. Fortunately, you aren't like most people. The power of the Slayer is a primal thing, an ancient force that is given to each Chosen One in turn, but the power itself never goes away. When a Slayer dies, the power still exists."

"It has its own groove," Buffy said, beginning to understand.

Willow raised the sword again and rested it on her shoulder. "You're groovier than most."

The breeze fluttered the candles again and their tiny flames danced but still did not go out. Willow's expression became suddenly very grim, all trace of humor gone. The time for procrastination, even for questions, was over.

"I'm going to bind you to that power, Buffy," she said. "I have to cut you a little and anoint you with your own blood. The blood of the Slayer, see? Even though it's your own, for the purposes of the spell it should still work. The spell isn't technically for that . . . it's really meant to let sorcerers see through the eyes of their ancestors. But it should make the pull of the primal power of the Slayer stronger than the pull of your physical form when you get where you're going.

"That means you'll have to concentrate on the moment in the past you want to return to, meditate on it with total focus. Once you've done whatever it is you need to do to stop all this from happening, you might not even remember any of this. 'Cause, y'know, it won't ever have happened."

An odd chill went through Buffy as she looked at Willow. "I don't want to forget," she said. "I think I need to remember this."

Willow shrugged. "What do I know? I'm just the travel agent."

Buffy took a long breath. "So where are you cutting?"

"Palm is pretty traditional."

The Slayer straightened up to her full height and held her hand out. Willow took it in hers and squeezed, then lifted the sword and lay it across Buffy's palm.

"Focus on that moment, the point in time you want to return to," Willow instructed. Then she slid the sword backward a fraction of an inch and the blade sliced through the rough skin. Buffy hissed air in through her teeth. Willow winced and glanced up at her apologetically.

"Look upon me as I draw seven drops of blood from you, blood which your ancestors have forfeited for you."

Blood welled up in Buffy's palm. Willow dropped the sword to the ground and took the Slayer's hand again. Cupping Buffy's hand in her left, Willow dipped the fingers of her right hand into the blood and then daubed Buffy's forehead and cheeks, then each of her wrists.

"Open your mouth," Willow said, voice weak.

Buffy did as she was told and Willow smeared her

mouth and teeth, even her tongue. The copper tang of her own blood was strong in the Slayer's mouth.

"From your heart, the blood of your ancestors, from the well of your spirit and the strength of all those who came before, I wed you to the ancient seed of the first among you, the first to bear the name Slayer, and each heart and soul and spirit 'tween she and thee. You are bound one to the other now, the power to the spirit."

Willow paused and for a second Buffy thought there was more. Then a shy smile crept over the features of the sorceress and she shrugged.

"I changed it around a little to make it fit, but that should cover it."

Buffy smiled. "It was great."

With her fingers pointed toward the ground, Willow began to swirl her hand in slow circles. The smoke from the candles and incense seemed suddenly drawn toward the center of the room and it gathered around Buffy, spinning lazily.

"That was the hard part," Willow said.

She gazed into Buffy's eyes, then went to the desk and picked up the small bundle of sticks. The smoke kept twisting around Buffy, though the Slayer could still feel the breeze from the windows. Willow held the bundle of sticks out to her and Buffy took them.

"When I nod, untie the ribbon and drop them," the sorceress said. "Good luck."

Buffy felt the prickly sticks and herbs in her hands, the slice in her palm stinging sharply. Her hand was slick with blood.

"In the name of Light and Darkness, in the name of the Earth and Air, in the name of the World and the Veil, remove thy curse and sting from this heart."

Willow gazed at her for a long moment and Buffy felt her eyes burn with the candle and incense smoke. Then Willow nodded, and the Slayer looked down at the bundle in her hands. She tugged at the red ribbon, felt its satiny fabric, and it came loose. Buffy watched the sticks fall . . .

. . . and fall . . .

*Falling.*

*And yet soon it seemed not like falling at all. Rather it was as though she were deep beneath some red and pulsing ocean, hurtling along with the force of a current of unimaginable power. Yet there was no resistance, no pressure upon her as she was propelled through this ocean. She was not some intruder, but part of this abyss, this void, this sea.*

*She was water in the torrent, wind in the storm.*

*A chasm of infinite black yawned before her, and yet it was somehow familiar to her. Once she had felt herself lost, forgotten her own identity. No more. She felt the pull of her flesh on her heart, as though that were where her soul resided. And in her gut, she felt another force tugging at her.*

*In the blackness around her, lights flickered. Souls. Sparks and thoughts and emotions. The bus station, where Willow, Xander, Oz and Anya fought against the Kakchiquels and bled to try to stop her.*

*Not her. Not Buffy, but Zotzilaha in her body.*

*Camazotz was there. And so was the beast inside Giles, the monster, the vampire. The Watcher was already dead.*

*The god of bats tore the spirit of his demon bride out of Buffy's body . . . and that hollow cavern of flesh was a vacuum. Its emptiness pulled her, tempted her heart, her spirit, to return to its rightful place.*

*No.*

*Buffy focused her mind on an earlier point. In her dorm room at U.C. Sunnydale, talking on the phone to Oz. Giles had asked her to track Willow down so that they might perform a spell that would locate Camazotz. She had a list of the materials he needed for the incantation. Yet when Oz told her that Willow was not home, Buffy had let it drop. Even knowing that Giles would be incensed, she had purposely not followed through.*

*For in her heart Buffy did not want Willow's help, or Giles's, or anyone's. She had convinced herself it was possible to separate the two lives she led. Not merely possible, but preferable. She had come to believe that letting her friends into her mission blurred the lines and detracted both from her efficacy as the Slayer and from the freedom and pleasure she ought to have had in her life as a nineteen-year-old college student.*

*Now she knew it had been selfish to think she should push them out of her life as the Slayer, and foolish to think that she could, that it was even possible to separate herself from her duty. But in that moment, she had allowed her emotions to cloud her reason. She and Wil-*

low had had a silly misunderstanding earlier, and things had been tense between them. Willow was avoiding her, and in that one, brief moment, Buffy had allowed herself to be petty enough to want to avoid Willow as well. When she had the chance to ask for Willow's help, to follow through, she let that petty tension stop her.

So that was the moment. She sensed it approaching, that time when she would be in her dorm room, on the phone with Oz, when she would make the mistake . . . the error that would lead to Giles's capture and eventual death and the horrors of the future she had just experienced.

She would reach out for that moment, join once more with her flesh, and she would change it, averting all that was otherwise to come.

Buffy focused.

Then, suddenly, images began to coalesce in the void around her and for a span that seemed eternal but might have been only a spark of time, she smelled the ocean and heard the ding of a distant buoy. She saw the harbor master's office. While Camazotz watched, the vampire clutched Giles in his talons, prepared to take his life.

In a moment she would flee, crash through the window to escape, and Giles would be taken away to die under the fangs of one of the bat-god's minions.

She had to stop it.

By instinct, Buffy reached out with her whole soul. But this was not the moment. She knew it. If she stopped here she would only repeat the same motions. If she surrendered to Camazotz, she and Giles would both die.

*Only by fleeing, surviving, did she have a chance to save him, and see what the future would bring then.*

*Recoiling, she tried to go on, tried to reach out, back to that moment on the phone with Oz, hours earlier that same night.*

*But she had lost her focus.*

*Every fiber of her soul cried out in alarm as she skipped past the designated hour, the day, the year . . .*

*In an instant that seemed very much like an eternity, Buffy reached out into the ether, the black-red void, and tried to grab hold of her own flesh, the body of the Slayer. A barrage of images assailed her and it was as though in that everlasting moment she could see through the eyes of every Slayer who had ever lived. This was what it meant that Willow's magick had bound her to the primal power of the Slayer.*

*Demon armies marched across frozen tundra. Villages burned. Horrors unimaginable died beneath her sword, her stake, her cudgel, her bare hands. Men draped in cloaks clutched magick in their grasp. Women in Victorian dress lay bloody in the streets. Dawn rose over ancient Rome and dusk fell across the French Revolution. She was all of them in a single instant. She hated their enemies and loved their lovers, she felt their pain and shared their bliss, and through every set of eyes she saw fangs, the face of the vampire, and the scattering of dust.*

*It was almost enough to pull her apart, to scatter her soul across the eons, among these thousands of years of Slayers.*

No, *she thought, and it echoed over millions of days, infinite moments. I am the Slayer.*

*Moment by moment, life by life, in an instant or a fraction of forever,* she pulled herself back. Heart and soul she grasped the lifeline that was the primal power of the Slayer and she found herself again, reached up through time and looked through her own eyes the moment she met her first Watcher, Merrick. The moment he died. The moment she first met Angel and the night they made love. All the times she laughed with Xander and cried with Willow, and all the times that Giles silently lent her his strength and faith.

Then she was there, in that moment again, in the dorm room as a ghost, staring down at her own self, at Buffy Summers on the phone, talking to Oz, about to make a terrible mistake. She reached out to touch her own face, to at last make things right, to join her own flesh.

*Collision.*

She could not enter. Willow had broken the spell Zotzilaha had cast, but it was that very enchantment that had twinned her to her own future soul. Now, in the past, she was unable to enter her body when it already had a soul.

All she could do was watch as Buffy . . . flesh and blood Buffy . . . said good-bye and hung up the phone.

The moment had passed. It was over.

She was lost.

And then, from the mist around her that was partially her dorm room and partially still the abyss, a voice called her name. Slowly a section of the mist began to coalesce into a familiar face, filled with affection but also deeply troubled.

"Lucy," Buffy said.

Once upon a time, this spirit too had been a Slayer. After death, she had lingered upon the ghost roads, where souls traveled to whatever final fate awaited them. Lucy was a guide to them, a lantern held high to light the way for those who became lost.

Just as Buffy was lost.

"How can this be?" the ghost of Lucy Hanover asked.

And Buffy told her, grateful that she was not alone.

# CHAPTER 7

In the house Oz shared with several other guys just off the U.C. Sunnydale campus, Willow struggled to keep all the cheese from sliding off the slice of pizza in her hands. Tendrils of it stretched from the slice to her teeth, still attached to the bite of pizza in her mouth. At last she severed the connection and the strings of cheese fell, nearly dragging all of it off the slice so that she had to use one hand to pull it up and plop it back down where it belonged. Her fingers were greasy and red with sauce and as she lifted it to take another bite, she caught Oz watching her.

He had paused in the process of eating his own slice and though he did not smile, his brows were knitted together in an expression of both curiosity and amusement.

"You could fold it," he suggested.

Willow saw that was exactly what he had done, his pizza folded in half like a paper airplane, keeping all the cheese and drippy sauce safely inside.

"I'm living dangerously," she told him. "Throwing caution to the wind. And pizza is supposed to be messy. The folding of pizza for one's own safety is an abomination."

Oz took a sip from the grape soda she had brought him, then gestured toward her with the can. "Plus, you got a big stack of napkins."

"Plus," she agreed, reaching for one off the pile. "But . . . even in the absence of napkins I would resist the urge to fold."

Oz nodded, clearly impressed. "Life without a net."

"It's my way," Willow said happily. She picked up her slice of pizza and bit into it. The cheese, completely loose now, began to slide off again and she was forced to keep the pizza in front of her face as she ate. Oz took two more quick bites of his slice, but he kept watching her.

This was exactly what Willow needed, just time with her guy. Buffy was her best friend and her roommate, but she had been more than tense lately and Willow felt as though she was being pushed away. It made her sad and a little angry at the same time, and hanging out with Oz and eating pizza was just what the doctor ordered.

In the corner of the room—surprisingly uncluttered for a guy's bedroom—sat Oz's guitar and amplifier.

"When we're done, will you play me that new song you've been working on?" she asked between bites.

"More a riff than a song, but if you insist."

"I do."

"So Buffy called while you were out."

Surprised, Willow put down her pizza and wiped her hands on a new napkin. "You didn't say."

"Didn't want to interrupt the feast. She and Giles are working on the Camazotz thing and were hoping you could search manifests, ports of call and such for ships stopped over in Sunnydale."

Instantly Willow's mind began to work, turning the request over, considering the time and difficulty involved. There were unknown variables, of course. She was not quite certain how to go about ascertaining which ships were currently moored in Sunnydale, but suspected it would be possible to find out.

"Did she say how fast they needed it? If it could help them find Camazotz, I guess it's important."

"Maybe. She didn't say."

Willow took a drink of her soda and pondered. The way Buffy had been behaving lately, trying to do everything herself, it was surprising that she would ask for help. *It* must *be important,* she thought.

"I should call her back."

But when she did, there was no answer. If Buffy had called while she was out, it could not have been more than twenty or thirty minutes earlier. A ripple of concern passed through her as the answering machine clicked on and she hung up without leaving a message. For a moment she just stared at the phone, then she picked it up again and began to dial the number for Giles's apartment.

A sudden squeal came from the amplifier in the corner of the room. Willow flinched at the assault on her eardrums and glanced over at the offending box to see that the red light that would have indicated it was on was not illuminated. Confused, she glanced at Oz, who seemed equally baffled. He rose and went to look at the amp and Willow had to hang up and start dialing again because she had lost her place.

The lights in the room dimmed as though the power were being siphoned away. In her peripheral vision, Willow saw something move. On the other end of the line, the phone in Giles's apartment began to ring. She turned, and there in the center of the room, just above the pizza box and the detritus of their little picnic on the carpet, the ghost of Lucy Hanover hung in the air, her transparent form shimmering with an ethereal light.

Willow hung up the phone. The grim cast of the specter's features sent a shudder through her.

"Were we expecting company?" Oz asked quietly.

"Lucy?" Willow ventured. "What is it?"

"*Good evening to you, friend Willow,*" the ghost began. "*I am sorry to interrupt, but we have little time, and it is not I who needs to speak with you.*"

She was about to ask what Lucy was talking about when she realized that there was another form coalescing there in the half-light of the room. Willow held her breath, wondering what this new ghost would be. It took form beside Lucy and even before the features of this spirit had become clear, a terrible knowledge formed in Willow's heart and she began to shake her head.

"No . . ." Willow whispered, shaking her head. "It can't be. You . . . you can't be . . ."

Oz came up beside her and slipped an arm around her waist. Willow was grateful, for she feared she might have collapsed otherwise.

"*Willow,*" the new arrival said, its voice like the rustling of the wind in the trees.

It was Buffy.

Willow felt cold and hollow inside. "Please, no. Buffy, tell me you're not—"

"*It isn't what you think, Will,*" the spirit said. A strange, tinny, static echo came from the powerless amplifier on the other side of the room. "*I'm me . . . sort of . . . but I've made a huge mistake and things are about to pretty much go to hell. I need your help to stop it.*"

"I don't understand."

"*When I called, I was supposed to ask you to come meet me and Giles to do a spell to find Camazotz . . . to go get the ingredients for the spell, but I . . .*" the apparition of Buffy became agitated. "*Look, I can explain it all later, but right now I need you to call Xander and Anya. They're at Giles's. Go pick them up and meet me at the harbor master's office in Docktown. And come armed. Heavily armed. Kakchiquels are stronger and faster than your average vamp and there are going to be a lot of them. Some Molotov cocktails wouldn't hurt.*"

Willow's heart was racing. She glanced at Oz.

"I can handle the Molotovs," he said simply.

"We'll be there," Willow told the phantom version of her best friend, whose form looked disturbingly similar to Lucy Hanover's. It was hard for her to shake the idea that both of them were ghosts, that Buffy was dead. "Are you really okay?"

"*With you guys to back me up, I will be,*" Buffy said

in that strange voice. *"But you have to hurry or it'll be just like last time."*

Willow frowned. "Last time?"

*"Giles will die,"* the Slayer told her. *"And that's just the beginning."*

*The pulsing abyss of red and black had given way now to a new void, a gray, swirling, formless mist. Buffy was familiar with this place, however. She had traveled here before, not merely as a spirit, but physically. These were the ghost roads. Silhouettes flitted through the nothingness all around her and low voices called out, some desperate and some filled with wonder.*

*Lucy led the way through the mists and Buffy followed as best she could, walking swiftly, though she knew that walking in this spirit realm was subjective.*

*"Stay with me,"* the ghostly Slayer said. *"We cannot afford to have you become lost if we are to prevent the events you described to me."*

*She reached one ethereal hand back. Buffy took it, and then they were traveling side by side. It chilled her to make this journey, to realize that though all souls experienced the time after corporeal death differently, many of them walked these paths and some got lost. For the fortunate ones, Lucy was there to guide the way.*

*"From what you have said, it seems I had a role in enabling Zotzilaha to trick you,"* Lucy continued. *"You have my regrets."*

*"For something you won't ever do?"* Buffy replied, trying to ignore the forms skittering about the gray ether*

around her. "Bygones. If you can get me back into my body, we'll call it even."

Lucy turned to her as they walked and smiled, her dark hair framing her porcelain features. "It won't be my doing, Buffy. I can aid you in manifesting for your fleshly self to see, but then it will be up to you to convince her to allow you to intrude. Just as, in your experience, what is yet to come at this time, Zotzilaha required your consent to touch your soul."

Before Buffy could respond, the mist around them parted and color bled back into the world. Everything seemed two-dimensional, false and thin, like the painted backdrop in an old movie. They were on the street in Docktown perhaps a block away from the harbor master's office. Somewhere nearby a dog was barking and the sound of the surf was a low undercurrent running beneath everything. The sky was somewhat overcast and the stars shone through only dimly. A gull cawed overhead.

Giles's weathered Citroën was parked only a few feet away. Though it was dark, Buffy could see herself sitting in the front seat.

"Come," Lucy said, and she drifted closer to the car.

Buffy followed the ghost until they stood just beside the front door, and now she could see the interior of the car more clearly. It was all wrong, the world inside out, being able to see herself from the outside like that. Her soul quaked and she yearned for the safety of her own flesh, the security of looking out from her own eyes. She was close enough now to see the expression on the face *of the Buffy inside the car, bored and frustrated, and only just beginning to wonder what was taking Giles so long.*

Giles. She turned and glanced along the street at the harbor master's office. A single light burned inside the small structure. On the front stoop, Giles stood, arms crossed impatiently. The sight of him there, alive and well, thrilled her, but there was no time to lose. Any moment now, she knew, the harbor master would drag him into the building where Camazotz was already waiting.

Lucy began to pass through the car as though it were not there at all and Buffy hesitated, her mind unable to grasp that such a thing was possible. She was merely a spirit now, her nineteen-year-old soul free of the limitations of flesh, but it was hard to imagine. Then Lucy reached out and grabbed her sleeve and tugged her into the car after her, and she found herself sitting in the backseat of the Citroën, staring at the back of her own head.

"Buffy," Lucy said, her voice clear and filled with authority.

Simultaneously, both soul and flesh turned to the ghost. In the front seat, Buffy's eyes widened in alarm and then she visibly calmed when she saw that it was Lucy Hanover who spoke to her. Then her gaze ticked to the right and she saw herself.

Buffy watched the shock and recognition in her own eyes.

"What are you supposed to be?" *the flesh and blood Buffy asked, steel in her voice, though her spiritual self could see how unsettled she was. No one else would have noticed, of course, but how could she not know herself.*

*"The ghost of Christmas yet to come," she replied. "Lucy told me . . . told you . . . something nasty was coming and that it would be your fault. It's true, but I can still stop it if you'll let me."*

*In the front seat, Buffy narrowed her gaze.* "How?"

*"Trust me."*

*For a moment, she feared it would not work, that all she had been through was for nothing. If she doubted, if she thought this was some kind of demonic trick, it would be over. But as Buffy reached out a spectral hand to touch her own face, she again saw recognition in her own eyes and she knew that there would be nothing barring her from entering her body this time.*

*Her fingers passed right through her skin.*

Once more, two souls merged as one in the body of the Slayer. Memories of the days to come, and the nightmarish future she had lived in so briefly, clashed with the mind of a Buffy who had yet to experience any of those things. Confusion overwhelmed her and she groaned and slumped down in the front seat of the car, felt the rough upholstery beneath her cheek.

Seconds ticked by, but no more than that. Her eyes focused on the dials of the radio and then she sat up again. Buffy was unsettled by this twinning of her soul, but at least part of her had felt it before, and so it was not quite as difficult.

In the backseat, the ghost of Lucy Hanover, less translucent in the darkness of the car, watched her curiously.

*"Are you all right?"*

"We'll find out," Buffy told her. "Make sure Willow and the others didn't get lost."

And then the ghost was gone.

Buffy leaned forward and peered out through the windshield at the harbor master's office. Giles was still there, but even now he reached up and knocked on the door again. She popped the door and jumped out. It hung open behind her as she ran toward him. Buffy was about to call out a warning when the door to the harbor master's office opened and a hand thrust out to drag Giles inside.

She cursed under her breath and ran faster, haunted by the familiarity of these events. The distant ring of a buoy reached her and dread crept through her as she began to fear that she could not change this moment. Every step was one she had taken before. The only difference now was her awareness of what lay behind that door, and of the Kakchiquels lurking in the shadows around the building, readying themselves to move in and surround the harbor master's office.

*No, there's one more difference,* she thought. *Help's on the way, and this time they know what they're dealing with.*

Xander sat on the floor in the back of Oz's van and held on to the box of Molotov cocktails as they took a hard corner. Glass clinked together in the box and he twitched. "Is there a reason I'm the one with the explosives between my legs?" he asked.

Willow was in the passenger seat next to Oz and she turned around to look at him, one hand propped on the dashboard as the speeding van turned another corner.

"They only blow up when you light them and throw them," she said helpfully.

"I knew that," he replied quickly. "But still, not the most comforting feeling in the world."

No one responded. The sense of urgency among them was grave, and no wonder. He was pretty puzzled by the whole Buffy-mirage thing Willow had told him about, but he'd seen weirder since the Slayer had moved to Sunnydale. What really bothered him was how much importance Willow and Oz were putting on Buffy's suggestion that they hurry. Xander did not like that at all.

He glanced around the back of the van, where Oz often carted his band's equipment around. Now the vehicle was loaded with weapons. No big war hammers, and no stakes. Going up against the Kakchiquels apparently required close quarters fighting without getting *too* close. There were two crossbows, an antique and a more modern version, a long sword, a battleax, and a curved blade Willow had said was a scimitar. If these guys were as fast as Buffy said, the crossbows would get used once and then things would get really ugly.

Anya sat across from him, a look of concern on her face. He loved her, but had not really wanted to bring her along.

"We did remember the lighter, right?" Willow asked suddenly.

Xander had a moment of panic before Anya proudly produced the silver metal lighter, popped it open and lit it. The flame was high and strong and only a few feet away from the Molotovs. He was about to protest when she snapped it shut.

"I'm very helpful," she told him. "Isn't it exciting?"

"Oh yes," Xander replied. He glanced down at the box of liquor bottles between his legs. Oz had made the Molotovs from booze his housemates had lying around. There had to have been an awful lot of it, because he'd been able to pick and choose just the alcohol that was one hundred proof or more, without which the little fire bombs would not work. Then he had ripped up an old bowling shirt and stuffed strips of cloth into the necks of the bottles. *A good job,* Xander thought.

Twelve bottles. He wondered how many vampires.

When the ghost appeared inside the van, he actually shouted in alarm. She was right between Xander and Anya, but he could still see his girlfriend through the dead Slayer's diaphanous form.

*"It has begun,"* Lucy Hanover told them. *"You must hurry."*

Much to Xander's dismay, Oz actually accelerated. They rounded one more corner and then were on the straightaway that shot through the center of Docktown right toward the ocean. At the end of the road was the harbor master's office. Though he was disturbed by the nearness of the dead girl's ghost, the crisis of the moment took precedence. Xander set the box of fire bombs aside and leaned forward to peer between Oz and Willow as the van careened down the street.

"No cops, no cops, no cops," he chanted.

There were no cops.

The street dead-ended at the ocean and it was dark down there, but he saw Giles's car on the left as they approached. And beyond it . . .

"Buffy," Willow said. "She just went into the building."

But Xander was not looking at the door to the harbor master's office. His attention was on the shadows on either side of the building. As he watched, the Kakchiquels appeared, their eyes sparkling orange in the dark, their dark tattoos making their faces barely visible. They slunk out from beside the building and began to gather in front of it in a kind of half-circle, facing the door.

"And here come the rest of the party guests," Xander said.

*"I will see if I can help,"* the ghost whispered.

Xander shivered, but when he turned to look at her again, Lucy was gone.

"Crossbows," Willow said, glancing back at him.

He grabbed the two weapons, made sure bolts were nocked into them, and handed them to Willow. She had one in either hand as Oz aimed the van straight at the front of the building.

"Anya." Xander used his foot to shove the box of Molotov cocktails at her. "Get ready to light a couple. We're going to need the vampires to cluster around us."

"Shouldn't be hard," Oz said simply. Then he laid a hand on the horn. "And now Buffy knows we're here."

At the roar of the engine and the sound of the horn, the vampires all turned. Oz steered right at them and two went down with a crunch of flesh and bone. Xander silently hoped they'd broken something significant enough that it would take a while for them to heal; at least long enough to keep them out of the fight.

Willow handed Oz a crossbow and they each fired out through their open windows. Xander heard a squeak of triumph from Willow and knew that they had both found their marks. Two Kakchiquels dusted.

Even as the front windows were being rolled up, vampires began to pound the sides and back doors of the van. The metal of the rear doors bucked and creaked, but were locked. Xander held a Molotov in each hand while Anya lit the alcohol-soaked strips of shirt that hung out of them as wicks. As soon as they flared up like torches he handed one to her and then slid to the back of the van.

"Anya, door," he said. "Oz, get ready to give me some room."

Oz put the van in gear. "Got it."

Xander tensed, raised his feet. "Unlock it."

Molotov blazing in her right hand, Anya popped the back lock with her left. The Kakchiquels were so intent upon battering the vehicle that it took a moment before they tried the handles again. The doors began to open and Xander kicked out with all his strength. They popped open, knocking several of the vampires aside.

Together, he and Anya hurled the flaming bottles into the crowd behind the van and vampires roared in pain as the Molotov cocktails shattered, spilling burning alcohol all over them. Four of them were set alight in an instant, their clothes igniting and their hair beginning to blaze. As those crumbled to the ground, trying to put themselves out, they blocked the others from attacking.

The passenger window shattered in front and hands reached in, clutching at air as they tried to reach for Willow. Xander did not need to tell Oz to drive. The van lurched forward, rolled thirty or forty feet, then slammed to a halt again.

Xander passed the battleax up to Oz and the scimitar to Willow. The sword he took for himself, though he had little proficiency with such a weapon. The back doors of the van swung open but no vampires approached, after what had happened to their comrades. Even as Willow and Oz got out, weapons in hand, Xander jumped out the back. Anya followed, sliding the box of Molotovs up to the edge. She pulled another out and lit it, even as the vampires began to attack again.

Anya threw the bottle, another Kakchiquel burned. Oz and Willow joined Xander in a rough circle, hacking at the monsters. As Xander watched, a greasy-haired vampire raked its claws across Oz's shoulder and he grunted in pain. Before he could go to Oz's help, Willow was there, her scimitar scything down to decapitate the vampire. More Molotovs shattered around them and vampires burned and turned to dust. Xander managed to down a couple of them, but not to kill them, and he cursed his clumsiness with the sword.

But he took them out of the fight. That's what counted.

A hand grasped his shoulder from behind, fingers digging in. Xander tore himself away, spun, and this time his blade did connect. Bone and muscle crunched but the sword's edge did not pass all the way through the vampire's neck. Sickly orange light burned in its eyes and though he had seen this breed of vampire once before, he was still unnerved by the bat tattoo on its face, seen so close up.

Then it dusted. Although he had not cut all the way through, apparently it had been far enough.

"And they say close only counts in horseshoes and hand grenades," he scoffed.

Behind him, Anya screamed. He turned to see two Kakchiquels grabbing at her. One of them was an olive-skinned woman with close-cropped hair and killer legs clad in leather pants. The other was a skinny guy with his hair in a ponytail. The female ripped an already lit Molotov out of Anya's hands.

Even as he moved to help her, Xander knew he would be too late. In his mind's eye, he had visions of Anya's neck being snapped.

Then the female vampire kicked her companion in the gut, causing him to stagger back, and she threw the Molotov. It burst into flames and the vampire tried to beat at his own chest even as his ponytail lit on fire, burning like a torch. He ran away as though he could escape it, and then exploded in a flash of cinders.

"What the—" Xander began, even as the vampire in leather pants turned to smile at him.

*"I said I would try to help,"* the Kakchiquel said in an eerie voice he instantly recognized.

Anya tried to attack the vampire and Xander had to stop her.

"No," he said. "It's Lucy Hanover."

"How's that?" Anya asked.

"I don't know, but I'm not complaining."

The three of them turned back to the fight. Fire blazed and blades fell and vampires died, and suddenly Xander realized they were winning.

The harbor master's office was trashed. Paperwork was strewn about the huge oak desk in the far corner. A lamp lay broken on the floor next to a phone that was off the hook. Both had been knocked off the desk. An old framed painting of a schooner about to crash onto the shore by a lighthouse hung nearly sideways on its hook. A shelf of books had been knocked over. Two other lights still burned in the room, dim, but leaving plenty of illumination to allow Buffy to see the horror that was unfolding before her.

The exact same scene she had been witness to before. Exactly the same.

In a narrow doorway that led into another part of the office, Giles lay half in one room and half in the other. His pants leg was torn and blood had begun to seep through the cloth. He tried to sit up, eyes glazed over as he shook his head, blinking rapidly. His face was already bruised and cut, blood dripping down his chin from some unknown wound inside his mouth.

The harbor master was hunched over Giles, holding him by the front of his shirt. With his other hand, the gray-bearded vampire gripped Giles's throat and snarled at Buffy.

*The same.*

But then, outside, she heard the loud beeping of a car

horn and the screeching of tires and she knew her friends had arrived. She was not in this alone.

"Let him go," Buffy demanded.

The vampire laughed, a deep, throaty, gurgling sound. "Or what? You'll kill me? And if I free him, what then? You'll let me go? We're not all that stupid, you know."

Words she had heard before.

With a grunt, the creature hauled Giles up and spun him around, holding him as hostage, as shield.

"Buffy . . . you must go . . ." Giles croaked.

The vampire rammed its head into the back of Giles's skull. The impact was loud, and sounded perilously fragile, as though something had broken. Buffy cringed and felt as though she might throw up. She had forgotten that part, that sound. Giles's eyes rolled up to white and he went limp in the vampire's powerful hands.

*Now,* she thought.

Buffy kept her eyes on Giles and the harbor master but she moved to the right, away from the door. Moments later, a hideous silhouette appeared in the doorway.

This Camazotz was a far cry from the bloated, pitiful beast he would become. Naked from the waist up, the tall, hideous thing was hunched over and his ravaged, skeletal wings jutted up from his back. On his chest was an enormous scar, and at the center of the scar an open wound that seemed partially healed, as though it might never close completely. Buffy had not understood that before, but she now knew the wound had come from his *feeding* of his Kakchiquels.

She had nearly forgotten what he looked like during

this, their first meeting, before his sanity had been lost to him. His hair was black and thickly matted, as was his long beard. He had a short, ugly snout with wet slits for nostrils, and his chalky, green-white skin was pock-marked all over. Upon his forehead were ridges that resembled those of a vampire. From his mouth jutted rows of teeth like icicles, and his fingers were inhumanly long and thin, white enough to have been little more than bones.

His eyes blazed orange fire.

"Join the party, Camazotz," she said amiably, her back to the wall now so that she could see both the demon-god and the vampire who held Giles's life in his hands.

The monster frowned at the familiarity in her voice. "You know me?"

"Better than you think."

The vestigial wings on his back fluttered with a dry whisper and Camazotz narrowed his blazing eyes.

"Those children outside. Friends of yours, I presume? They're going to die, you know."

Of course he had seen Willow, Xander and the others fighting his Kakchiquels as he entered the building. She figured he had dismissed them. They were mere humans, after all, and young at that.

"I think they might surprise you," Buffy told him.

Out of the corner of her eye she watched the harbor master, just in case. Camazotz noticed.

"The man means something to you," the demon-god said, indicating Giles. "Your Watcher?"

The same words.

His voice was wet and thick, something trapped in quicksand and desperate to be free. Again her gaze ticked toward Giles, still unconscious, and back to Camazotz.

"Not my Watcher. A friend," she admitted. She hefted the stake in her right hand, turned its point toward him. Though she had no desire to contribute to the way the scene was repeating itself, she could not help taunting him. After all, she already knew his sore spots.

"So you're the god of bats, huh? Considering the job description, those are pretty pitiful wings."

Camazotz actually flinched.

"The wife caught you napping, huh?" She gestured with the stake at his back. "Can you even fly with those?"

Camazotz lost all of the cool reserve he'd shown, and a primitive snarl split his features. His eyes flared and sparked.

"I knew I would have to destroy you to reach the Hellmouth, cow. I am prepared. My Kakchiquels are bred and raised by me. They do not fear you, girl, because they have never *heard* of you. They will face you without hesitation, down to the last of them, because they do not know what a Slayer is."

"Yeah, yeah. I've heard it all before," she replied, returning his snarl as she relaxed and tightened the grip on her stake. She stared at him, letting the moment of silence charge the air between them with crackling energy. Then she smiled. She knew she would not be able to antagonize him into attacking her, but she had to try.

"Let's get it on, stumpy."

The flesh of the ancient creature seemed almost to

ripple with his rage. He shuddered, nostrils flaring, long needle teeth bared, and he rose up to his full height, about to lunge at her.

Then Camazotz smiled.

Buffy sighed softly, resolved to play it out, praying that the small changes she had wrought on this night would be enough to buy her the moment she needed.

"You want to antagonize me into direct combat, believing you can destroy me and still save your . . . friend," Camazotz said, slippery voice tinged with wonder. "And maybe you would at that, Slayer. Maybe you would. But I have—"

"Walked upon the earth since before the human virus blah blah blah. I remember. Just get on with it."

Camazotz stared at her, obviously unnerved that she had spoken the very words that had been about to come from his mouth. His chest rose and fell as he studied her. Then he gestured to the harbor master.

"If she does not obey me instantly, kill him. *Drink* him." Tongue flicking out over his teeth, Camazotz glared at her. All trace of humor was gone from his horrid countenance. "Throw the stake down. On your knees and crawl to me."

# CHAPTER 8

**O**n your knees and crawl to me.

So there it was. The same moment, the same situation. Even as the seconds had ticked toward those words, this very instant, she had been turning it over in her mind, examining it, trying to see if there was anything she could have done differently. If she had not broken into the office, Giles would already be dead. If she had charged the harbor master, Giles might already be dead. If she had attacked Camazotz as he entered, the harbor master would have killed Giles immediately. And now . . .

If she did as Camazotz commanded, she and Giles were *both* dead. If she attacked, Giles would be savaged, possibly murdered, before she could reach him. Now, though, she knew that even if she fled, she would be saving only herself. Camazotz was keeping Giles alive for the moment to try to manipulate her, but she had lived this night before and she knew that if she ran,

Giles would become something even more horrible than the god of bats himself.

Buffy would not surrender herself, but she had to buy time and hope that her friends came through for her. She had to trust in them. In the vampiric old man's grasp, Giles moaned softly, beginning to regain consciousness. Camazotz stared at her, almost daring her to attack. When she dropped to her knees on the wooden floor, his horrid, inhuman face split into a grin that revealed the rows of needle teeth within once more. A thin line of spittle ran into the matted hair on his chin.

"Now crawl," the demon-god sneered.

On her knees, Buffy stared up at him. Her heart played out a rapid, erratic rhythm and she held her breath. Seconds passed and the energy that sparked in Camazotz's eyes seemed to burn brighter as he grew furious.

"Crawl!"

Buffy did not want to crawl. She put the stake carefully on the floor beside her, praying she would have a chance to use it. Reluctantly, she went down on all fours and began to crawl toward Camazotz.

Out of the corner of her eye, Buffy saw his lackey, the harbor master, relax the hold he had on Giles.

"Buffy, no . . ." Giles murmured weakly.

The god of bats began to laugh.

From the open doorway, the blade of a scimitar swept toward his neck. In the last moment, he sensed or heard his attacker and began to turn, and the curved blade sank into the putrid flesh of his chest.

Eyes wide with fear and shock at what she had just

done, Willow tried to pull the blade from Camazotz's body but it was lodged there. The demon-god screamed in rage and shook her loose. Willow staggered back two steps.

The white-haired vampire gaped at the spectacle of his master reeling, trying to pull the scimitar from his chest. Buffy snatched up the stake from the floor and leaped across the room at him. Giles saw her coming and tried to duck but the vampire held him firmly. The harbor master looked up at Buffy at the last moment, but then she had him. With a short kick, she broke one of his arms and Giles staggered free, still unsteady on his feet.

Shock registered on the harbor master's face as Buffy grabbed him by the throat and rammed the stake through his heart. He crumbled to dust even as she spun away to see Camazotz tear the scimitar from where it was wedged in the bones of his chest. The demon-god roared and hunched toward Willow.

"Hey!" Buffy shouted.

As Camazotz turned toward her, he faltered, unsteady from the wound Willow had given him.

"Where were we?" the Slayer asked. "Oh, yeah, you were gonna crawl?"

The god of bats glared at her with such hatred that Buffy shuddered. But the electric flicker of demonic energy in his eyes had dimmed. He was off-balance, weakened, and apparently the last thing he wanted was to face the Slayer now.

"It was not supposed to be like this," Camazotz muttered.

Buffy started toward him. "Sucks to be you."

Then, as she and Willow both watched in surprise, Camazotz turned and with a burst of renewed strength, leaped up onto the desk and crashed through the window and onto the street beyond.

"No!" Buffy yelled as she ran to the window.

But when she stared down at the pavement in the alley on the side of the building, there was only shattered glass and broken bits of window frame. Camazotz was gone.

"I must say," Giles began weakly as he walked up behind her, "for a moment there . . ."

Buffy turned to him and smiled, shaking her head. Giles had long scratches on his face and neck, a small cut on his forehead that had bled quite a bit, and he hissed in pain as he reached up to touch the spot on the back of his skull where the harbor master had struck him.

"You're a mess," she told him.

"Yes. Well, you don't have to be so happy about it," Giles replied tiredly. He glanced around. "Have you seen my glasses?"

They were on the floor several feet away. She grabbed them and handed them to him, just as Willow called to her.

"Buffy! Out front!"

Together they ran to the door, but when they reached it they were surprised to see Xander, Oz and Anya just up the street, standing by the van and watching in astonishment as the six or seven remaining Kakchiquels fled into the shadows. Bruised and bloody, Xander nevertheless began to give chase.

"Come on!" he cried. "'Tis but a scratch!"

He ran out of steam after half a dozen steps and bent over, hands on his knees, trying to catch his breath.

"Come back and fight, ya bunch of yellowbellies," he rasped.

"Yellowbellies?" Oz asked.

Xander shrugged. "It's a John Wayne thing."

Buffy lent Giles her support as they walked down the steps with Willow. On the street, the others gathered around them. Anya threw her arms around Xander and kissed him passionately until he winced and gingerly began to search his rib cage for some hidden damage.

"Camazotz got away," Willow announced.

"Oh, that's perfect," Anya snapped. "So much for urgent. Xander and I didn't even have time to make Giles's bed. We rush all the way down here, put our lives on the line, waste all that alcohol on fire bombs, and you let him get away."

"Well, *let* is a strong word," Willow said defensively.

Anya crossed her arms and glared at them sternly.

"If it helps any, Willow has impeccable timing and probably saved my life and Giles's," Buffy offered.

But Giles was paying her little attention. He was staring at Anya with a baffled expression on his face. "What about my bed?"

"So!" Xander said abruptly. "How're we gonna find this guy now?"

"Actually," Buffy replied, "I think I know just the person to ask. But we're going to need Lucy's help."

"Ooh, she was so great," Willow said excitedly. "She

possessed a vampire, this trashy girl in leather pants, and was helping us out." She glanced around. "Where'd she go, anyway?"

Xander and Anya turned to stare expectantly at Oz. He stood there with his hands in his pockets and raised his eyebrows as if he had no idea why they were looking at him.

"Oz?" Giles inquired.

"He dusted her," Xander explained.

"You killed her?" Willow asked, horrified.

Oz shrugged. "Accidentally. And, not that I'm not sorry but, last I checked, ghosts pretty much already dead."

"Yeah, but ouch." Buffy shivered and then looked around at her friends, these people without whom she would not have been able to survive this night a second time. She had no idea what she would have done without them. Still, the night was not over yet.

"Come on," she said, heading for Giles's car. "We've got work to do."

Giles lay on the couch and stared around at his apartment. It had never seemed so small to him. The clock ticked the seconds off loudly on the wall and he could not keep his gaze from straying to it from time to time. It was a quarter till midnight and he did not think he had ever seen Buffy and her friends so quiet. The calm was almost enough to make it seem as though the conflict with Camazotz was over.

But the final battle was still to be fought.

They had returned an hour and a half before but it had

taken time for them to cleanse their wounds. Oz had a gash on the back of his head that might need stitches. Giles had washed his own scratches and cuts with alcohol and tried not to whimper loud enough for the others to hear. He would probably have a small scar on his forehead from the harbor master's initial attack, but it would be a near thing. They were all suffering from bruises and aches that would linger for days afterward, but were fortunate that none of their injuries were more serious.

Xander and Anya were curled up together on the floor . . . which was preferable to Giles's bed, as far as he was concerned. He thought Xander might even be snoring lightly. Willow and Oz were at the table poring through books to make absolutely certain the spell that had to be cast would be powerful enough for their purposes. But there was really no way to be sure.

Buffy had placed candles all about the room. There had not been enough white ones so she had been forced to improvise with a small box of birthday candles. Now the Slayer moved quietly from place to place with a silver lighter Anya had given her and lit the candles one by one.

With the corner of his shirt, Giles wiped the lenses of his spare glasses—the others had been cracked—and then slipped them on. He approached Buffy as she lit the last of the candles and when she turned to face him her eyes brightened. It warmed his heart to see the affection she felt for him, but it seemed odd, too, for she behaved as though she had not seen him in months.

"There's a great deal you're not telling me," he said, his voice low.

Buffy nodded. "Pretty much."

"You seem different."

"Older?"

*Curious,* Giles thought. "Actually, I only meant that you seem like your old self again. Your behavior earlier tonight, well, you seemed impatient and quite rash."

The Slayer only raised her eyebrows. "Yep. You ready?"

Frustrated, Giles refused to allow her to brush him off. "How do you know all of this? About Zotzilaha and Camazotz? Do you really expect Willow to be able to learn alchemy in a matter of hours? How can you be certain the references to gold being Camazotz's weakness are true?"

His mouth opened again but Giles fell silent, embarrassed by his outburst.

A sadness washed over Buffy's features, but it lasted only a moment. "You just have to trust me. And believe in Willow."

That flustered him. "I do, on both counts. But alchemy? Surely there's another, simpler way to find something gold to use against Camazotz. Some weapon."

Buffy raised an eyebrow. "You have a golden dagger around?"

"Well, no, but—"

"Want Willow and me to raid our mothers' jewelry, maybe break into some jeweler's downtown?"

"Of course not! But perhaps if we had enough gold to melt down we could simply *coat* a dagger with it, or a stake for that matter, rather than having a weapon made of solid gold."

"I can't be sure something that wasn't solid would work, but let's say it would. What temperature does gold have to be at to melt?"

Giles glanced away. "Nearly two thousand degrees Fahrenheit."

"Do you know of a working foundry nearby where we could get a furnace up to *two thousand* degrees? Y'know, *right now?*"

"No. Certainly not. But look at it from my perspective, Buffy. In all my years researching the supernatural I have never once seen anyone successfully complete an alchemical process."

"I'm not surprised," Buffy said. "But I know Willow can do it."

The Slayer smiled softly, the flicker of candlelight on her face. Giles did not think he had ever seen her look so tired.

Buffy turned away and clapped her hands together, rousing Xander and Anya and drawing the attention of Willow and Oz at the table. "All right, let's evict the Mayan deities from Sunnydale so we can get some sleep. I still have to figure out how I'm going to convince Professor Blaylock not to fail me.

"Willow, are we ready?"

The young witch nodded. "Giles had all the things we needed to perform the spell. No guarantees, but I'm thinking it'll hold the big stinkin' liar of a Prophet."

"She's channeling her ire," Oz added.

"And we're all grateful," Buffy said gravely. "Now if Lucy isn't too cranky after you cut her head off, this just might work."

Once again, Buffy had the feeling that events were repeating themselves, though in this case the circumstances were not exactly the same. They were in Giles's apartment, for one, and it was night. More importantly, this time around, Giles was with them, safe and sound save for a few scratches and knocks on the head. He had a hard skull, though, her former Watcher. He'd survived plenty of cranial trauma before.

They were all tougher than she had been willing to give them credit for. And they were all here, and alive. Giles. Xander. Anya. Somewhere, Faith still lay in a coma. And down in Los Angeles . . . Angel. Their destinies lay ahead of them, whatever the future might hold, but for now Buffy had prevented the dark fates that had been in store for all of them, for the world. She had her friends again.

Still, though, there was much work to be done.

The candles she had placed in a rough circle around the room burned with white-orange flames that seemed to sway in a breeze that came from nowhere. Buffy and Willow sat opposite one another at either end of Giles's table. Xander, Anya, Oz and Giles completed the circle. It was a sloppy séance, or summoning, or whatever the official name for it was, but they did not have time to worry about the niceties of such things. Buffy wanted to bring an end to things tonight.

"Clear your minds," Willow instructed.

Her voice seemed somehow different to Buffy, deeper, more confident. It took her only a moment to realize that it was the same as the voice of her older self, that future sorceress who wielded her authority with as much grace as she did her magick.

Willow's eyes snapped open, fixed directly on Buffy. "I said clear your minds."

"Oh," Buffy said sheepishly. "Sorry."

Same words. But no longer the same situation. She had altered the past and so changed the future, yet Buffy would not rest until Camazotz was destroyed. Only then would she truly believe it was over.

Eyes now closed, Buffy took a long, deep breath, let it linger within her for a moment, and then let it out as though it were her very last. It was a cleansing, meditative technique Giles had taught her way back during sophomore year of high school. It worked.

"With hope and light and compassion, we open our hearts to all those walkers between worlds who might hear my plea and come to aid us in this dark hour," Willow began, intoning the words slowly.

Buffy felt Xander's hand grip hers on one side, and Oz do the same on the other. It was as though the innate power within Willow, the peace and mystic qualities within her heart and soul that made her so naturally attuned to the energies of the supernatural, had created a kind of electrical charge that ran through them all—a circuit of benevolent magick, a beacon to the souls to whom Willow now spoke.

"Spirits of the ether, bear my voice along the paths of

the dead, whisper my message to every lost soul and wanderer," Willow continued, voice lowering in timbre, becoming not unlike a kind of chant. "I seek the counsel of Lucy Hanover, she who was once a Slayer. She who holds high the lantern to light your path on the journey between worlds."

After half a minute's silence, Willow spoke again, this time her voice barely rose above a whisper. "Lucy, do the lost ones bring my voice to you?"

The answer was immediate.

*"That hurt."*

Buffy opened her eyes. The others were all looking as well. Lucy Hanover was there, hovering over the center of the table they had created, staring down at Oz with an admonishing look on her ghostly face.

Oz glanced away, looking a bit chagrined. "Sorry."

The candles flickered in the room and the shadows danced, the variations in light washing over and through the ghost. Parts of her misty form seemed more transparent than others. Normally reserved, Lucy smiled.

*"All is forgiven. The heat of battle, after all, and all those vampires around. To be honest, it did not really hurt overmuch. I was merely controlling that form, not . . . not living in it."*

Buffy felt sorrow for Lucy, then. She had been bodiless for a time, a lost soul in some ways, but she had flesh and blood to return to. She could not imagine what it must be like to be truly dead.

*"Good evening once more, Willow,"* Lucy said. *"I am pleased you are unhurt."* Then the ghost turned her dark

eyes upon Buffy. *"We meet again, Slayer. I believe I know why you have called upon me once more. You wish me to try to lure The Prophet here, to mislead and help entrap her?"*

"If that's all right with you," Buffy replied.

*"Oh, it's fine,"* Lucy told her, a smile on her ghostly features. *"Better than fine. The creature perpetrated a horrible cruelty upon you, and facilitated a hideous future. We have the opportunity to prevent that, and to punish her for her evil deception."*

"Spoken like the Slayer you are. Thank you." Buffy glanced at the table. Upon it lay a snow globe from Aspen someone had given to Giles, a seemingly harmless item. Around it, Willow had laid black yarn in an ever shrinking circle, its inner end beneath the base of the globe.

"Anyway, I don't think you'll have trouble with her," Buffy told the phantom Slayer as she watched the candlelight flicker off the globe. All was still inside it at the moment. "Zotzilaha wants to come."

"She wants your body," Xander observed happily.

Buffy shot him a look and then glanced back up at Lucy.

Lucy seemed almost to bow, though it might merely have been a wavering of whatever ethereal substance comprised her body. "I will seek her." Then, as if she had never been there at all, she was simply gone.

Oz was the first to break the circuit. He let go of Buffy's hand and then Buffy released her grip on Xander's. Anxiously, she glanced beneath the table to be sure the circle of salt Willow and Anya had laid out there was still intact and unbroken.

Though she had felt relieved when Giles had been saved, and quite calm as they prepared for this moment, now that it had come Buffy began to grow agitated again. In her mind's eye she could still recall the pain of Zotzilaha's touch, the terror she had felt as the curse the thing had used upon her became apparent. It chilled her and a sickly feeling began to churn in her stomach.

This was the creature who had started it all, who had stolen her body. Camazotz was a horrifying thing and he had to be stopped, but Zotzilaha was in some ways even more insidious. It occurred to Buffy for the first time since she had saved Giles that there was no longer an echo within her, no more twin soul. She was herself again, whole and complete and alone in that corporeal shell. But she still could feel the cold touch of this thing they had now summoned and she felt tainted by it.

She was the Slayer, and she had all of her friends around her, yet some small part of her was still afraid.

Oz broke the silence. "Well," he said. "That was bracing."

"What now?" Xander gazed at Buffy, sort of nodding his head to prod her to answer the question. His eyebrows went up as further punctuation. "Buff?"

"We wait—"

A gust of wind cut through the room fast and hard enough to scour the walls. Impossibly, though the flames sputtered, the candles still burned. Then, in a single moment, every candle in the roof was snuffed.

The wind swirled tighter and tighter until it no longer touched them, instead creating a miniature tornado in the center of the table. Then the wind itself seemed to bleed an oily black, the oil to spread and flow and take form. The wind slowed.

It *became* something.

*"She has agreed to speak with you."*

Buffy glanced quickly toward the window and saw the ghost of Lucy Hanover, hovering there, watchful. Wary. Knowing.

When she looked back, the wind had died and the flowing black core of it had coalesced into a figure, the silhouette of a woman. Zotzilaha had no face that Buffy could see, nor flesh, not even the diaphanous mist that gave Lucy shape. Instead, The Prophet was like a female-shaped hole in the room, a black pit that lingered in the air like soot from a smokestack.

But it spoke. *She* spoke.

*"Slayer. You summoned me. How may The Prophet be of service?"*

Her voice was like the whisper of a lifelong smoker whose throat had been ravaged by cancer. Pained and ragged and knowing, in on the perversity of the joke.

*Gotcha,* Buffy thought.

"You can tell me where Camazotz is, and then you can go away, pretty much forever, *Zotzilaha*."

The thing twitched, her obsidian form shimmered where it hung in the room, a wound between worlds.

*"I do not know how you found me out,"* the demon-spirit said, *"but you are of no use to me now. Fortunate for you. I will depart."*

Willow stood up from the table. "No. I don't think you will."

Buffy felt a tiny pang of alarm when the blackness began to flow toward Willow, menace in the way it seemed to consume reality around it. But then it collided with the invisible barrier created by the salt beneath the table and the spell Willow and Giles had performed, and the pulsing void began to pool and bleed around the edges of the table.

*"What have you done?"* the demoness thundered.

*"They have trapped you, false seer, cruel spirit,"* Lucy Hanover said, floating toward the table now.

Buffy stood up as well. "Where is he? I know you are still linked to him or he wouldn't be able to track you. How far can you run away from someone you're bound to forever?"

The blackness quivered and at last seemed to take a more female shape. There might even have been a face there, vaguely outlined, somehow beautiful in its hatred for them.

*"Camazotz sailed to your shores in the belly of a vessel called* Quintana Roo, *a vessel that is now moored in the harbor not far from here. I care not what becomes of him. Now free me, Slayer."*

Buffy furrowed her brow. "Like that's gonna happen."

Even as the demon-spirit began to protest, Willow and Giles spoke simultaneously, their words overlapping as Zotzilaha screamed at them in fury. Once more that insidious, amorphous darkness began to churn, a tornado made of oil and tar that spun in upon itself, faster and faster around the center of the table. Around the snow globe. Tiny white flakes began to swirl in the glass ball and the flowing sable twisted tighter in upon itself, following the diminishing circles created by the black yarn beneath it.

With a sound like grease burning, Zotzilaha was gone. The inside of the snow globe was completely black, as though it were filled with ink. It was going to make an interesting paperweight for Buffy's dorm room.

Buffy stared at the globe. "Bet you didn't see that coming," she said. "Hell of a Prophet *you* are."

# CHAPTER 9

For the second time that night, Willow rode shotgun while Oz drove to Docktown, once again with Xander and Anya in the back of the van. Some of the students she had met at U.C. Sunnydale who came from out of state had been surprised to find how chilly it could get in Southern California at night, but Willow had lived here all her life. Though they had swung by Xander's for some things, there had been no time to go back to the dorm and Willow regretted that now. A cold wind blew through the shattered window on her side and she shivered, lost in her thoughts.

"So, who else thinks Buffy's acting kind of freaky?" Xander asked from the back.

"I have always considered her somewhat freakish, so I'm not sure I could tell the difference," Anya replied.

"Freak-y, not freak-ish," he corrected.

Anya averted her gaze and was silent.

The van rumbled on toward Docktown and no one else replied. Normally that would not have stopped Xander, but tonight it did. He said nothing more about it. Willow was glad. Though she had a great many thoughts of her own about Buffy's behavior that night, they were not really things she wanted to discuss. It was all so odd.

How did she know so much about Camazotz and Zotzilaha? How had Buffy appeared in Oz's house as a spirit? How had she known the very moment when Giles's life would be in jeopardy, and that Camazotz and his Kakchiquels would be there?

Even as these questions whirled in her mind, they arrived at the wharf. As Buffy had requested, Oz parked back from the docks, out of sight of the ships that were moored there. Giles pulled in behind them a moment later with Buffy in the passenger seat. They all piled out quickly, but as quietly as possible. As the others began to remove the weapons from the back of Oz's van and from the trunk of Giles's car, Willow stood near the front of the van and stared at the stretch of ocean she could see between large shipping warehouses.

The sea was dark and almost invisible in that blackness, but even blind she would have known where she was. The sound of the surf and the scent of the ocean, the cool salty dampness that hung in the air, were all unmistakable. As Willow took it all in, she heard the scuff of a sole upon the pavement behind her and turned to find Buffy watching her, a massive compound bow in her hands. A quiver of arrows hung across her back along with a sword, whose heavy scabbard was tied to a leather thong the Slayer had slipped over her shoulder.

"Hey," Buffy said gravely. The infectious exhilaration she had exhibited earlier had dispersed, and now she was as intense as she had ever been.

"Hey," Willow replied, watching her best friend with concern.

"So you're all set for the spell?"

A wave of uncertainty went through Willow and she shrugged lightly. "I read that alchemy text by Saint Germain and I memorized the spell that seemed like the one you described. But I told you, Buffy. I tried it earlier and it doesn't work. Giles doesn't believe it *will* work."

From where they stood, Willow could hear the wood of the wharves creaking with the ebb and flow of the ocean. In the darkness, the constant blink of a buoy light drew her attention but she forced herself to keep her eyes on Buffy. If the Slayer was right, and gold was Camazotz's one true weakness, their success might depend on her ability to do this spell.

"Giles is wrong," Buffy said simply. "You can do it. As long as you know the secret."

Panic shot through Willow then and her heartbeat sped up. "Which I don't," she said. "I vote for chopping Camazotz into tiny pieces. I gave him a pretty good whack earlier myself. And there was blood! Tiny pieces is a good plan."

Willow would never forget the knowing smile Buffy gave her then. Though it only confused her more, it also helped to dispel the rising panic in her.

"Tiny pieces is Plan B," Buffy said. "Camazotz isn't an ordinary monster, Will. God of bats, remember? Ancient Mayan deity. The tiny pieces strategy would take him out of the game for now, but he could easily come back again later."

"And probably would," Willow admitted. "Mainly 'cause being chopped into tiny pieces tends to annoy the deities."

"That it does," Buffy agreed. "You can do this, Will. You can."

"As long as I know this secret that I don't know."

"I do."

Willow stared at her.

"It won't work if you're doing it for personal gain," Buffy said.

"That makes sense," Willow admitted. "But back at Giles's place, I wasn't doing it for me. I was doing it 'cause you told me to."

"But in the back of your mind, you had to be aware that a big hunk o' gold could buy a lot of hats and shoes."

A twinge of guilt went through Willow. "And books. Don't forget books. But that's not fair. I mean, I wasn't really doing it for personal reasons. How can you not at least be aware of the potential value of gold when gold is what you're trying to make?"

Buffy offered a small smile in return. "Now you see why no one believes in alchemy."

"So how am I supposed to do this spell?"

"When the moment comes, you'll do fine."

"I'm glad you have faith in me, but what if you're wrong?"

Buffy glanced past her, toward the vehicles. "If I'm wrong, it looks like we're prepared for Plan B."

Over at the van, the others were almost completely geared up. Everyone wore black except Oz, who was still in the New York Yankees game shirt he had been wearing earlier. Xander had a pillowcase over his shoulder that made him look like the biggest kid in the neighborhood out trick-or-treating. Anya cradled a pair of crossbows as though they were an infant whose diaper she did not want to change. Oz and Giles carried the weapons they had all used earlier.

The sword that hung across Buffy's back was different. In the shadows of the night, Willow had not recognized it at first, but now she had a glimpse of the scabbard and saw that it was the same sword with which Buffy had stabbed Angel more than a year before.

"I thought you were never going to use that sword again."

"It seemed appropriate tonight. And it goes with what I'm wearing."

The Slayer began to turn, but Willow called her name and Buffy paused to regard her again.

"There's a lot I don't understand," Willow told her. "And I know you're being Coy Woman for a reason. But tell me this much: the secret to alchemy. How do you know that?"

Buffy smiled. *"You* told me."

\* \* \*

The *Quintana Roo* was moored at the farthest end of the wharf from the harbor master's office, in front of an old warehouse that had been gutted by fire years before and never repaired. She was a cargo ship registered in Mexico but owned by a Guatemalan export company that had gone under the year before. All of that Willow had been able to discover with a quick search of records online.

Buffy had no idea if the ship had been bought or the owners and crew slaughtered, but at this point the question was moot. Though her hull was scarred and plated from numerous repairs and she barely looked seaworthy, the *Quintana Roo* had made it to Sunnydale with the dark prince of the Mayan underworld and his minions on board. In mythology, the demon-god presided over a house of bats, and Buffy could still remember that dark future time when Camazotz had been chained in a dank basement where bats hung overhead. She had a sense that if Camazotz were on board, licking his wounds, he would be in the cargo hold.

But she was prepared for that.

Waves crashed the pilings beneath the wharf and one long end of a rope the ship was tied off with slapped against the side of the vessel with the rising of the wind. The wharf and the *Quintana Roo* both creaked loudly as they leaned together, as if whispering the pains of their age to one another. The overcast sky had mostly cleared and the stars shone down, but the moon was only a crescent, torn in the ceiling of the night.

Despite its stated purpose for docking in Sunnydale,

there were no crates on the wharf beside the *Quintana Roo*, nor any evidence that even an attempt had been made to unload any cargo. Buffy was not surprised. Camazotz might be an archaic leftover from a bygone age, but he had been crafty enough to have one of his Kakchiquels turn the harbor master into a vampire rather than simply killing him. They didn't have to unload any cargo, or even pretend to, if they had him on their side.

But the harbor master was dust now. And as far as Buffy was concerned, in the morning the *Quintana Roo* would just be another mystery for the local authorities.

In the shadow of another ship, the *Sargasso Drifter*, Buffy gathered her forces—her friends—about her. With a single glance she let them all know that silence was a necessity. Carefully she slipped between stacks of cargo crates from the *Sargasso Drifter* and then glanced up the wharf at the *Quintana Roo*.

As she suspected, there were sentries posted on either side of the metal gangplank that led from the deck down to the dock. They stood with their arms crossed, straight and solid.

One of them turned to look toward her. Buffy did not move, unwilling to give herself away, and the sentry looked away again. He had not seen her. But Buffy had recognized him. He had a pug nose and a shaved head and once upon a time she had thought of him as Bulldog. The other guard was a female and Buffy could see now that save for the black bat tattoo around her eyes, the guard's features were painted white.

*Clownface,* Buffy thought. *And Bulldog. I'd almost forgotten about you two.*

She stiffened. A part of her wanted very badly to take these two Kakchiquels down hand to hand. But that was not part of the plan. And, after all, she had dusted them once before, hadn't she? In that dark future world?

Buffy glanced back among the stacked cargo crates at her friends and found them all watching her expectantly. Aside from Buffy herself, Giles and Willow had the best aim, so she had armed them both with crossbows. Anya had the scimitar Willow had used earlier, Oz an ax and Xander a sword. If they were lucky, they would not have a chance to use them.

Silently, she withdrew a few steps from the open stretch of wharf and signaled to Willow and Giles. As planned, they slipped off through the cargo, away from the water and toward the burned-out warehouse. Buffy then gestured for the others to come forward. There were no jokes from Xander, no protests from Anya. No one made a sound.

Buffy slid along the crates again and peered around the edge of the stack. Clownface and Bulldog still stood guard at the gangplank. Up on the deck of the *Quintana Roo,* nothing moved. Buffy reached up and slid a single arrow from the quiver on her back. Most arrows bore metal tips but these were all wood. She fitted the notch at the back of the arrow to the bowstring, took aim and waited.

Patience was the order of the evening. Patience, and silence.

A sudden loud bang echoed inside the ruined warehouse.

Bulldog and Clownface both glanced around immediately. They conferred in whispers and then Bulldog began to walk toward a boarded-up door in the dilapidated structure. He moved like a predator, ready to pounce at any moment.

When Bulldog was perhaps a dozen feet from the front of the building, Buffy whistled at Clownface. The vampire's head whipped toward the piles of cargo crates where Buffy and the others hid, then she glanced at Bulldog. Uncertainty clouded Clownface's features. She turned toward Buffy.

That was all the Slayer had been waiting for. She drew back the string on the compound bow and let the arrow fly with such force that it went all the way through Clownface and *thunked* into a wooden piling behind the vampire. Her white-painted eyes went wide and she glanced down at the small hole in her chest even as she disintegrated, her ashes swept away by the ocean breeze.

Buffy glanced over to see Bulldog six feet from the door. At the sound of her arrow striking wood, he lifted his head slightly. Before he could turn, a crossbow bolt shot between two slats in the boarded-up door and Bulldog was dust as well.

"Yes," Xander whispered behind her.

With a grin, Buffy put a finger to her lips to shush him, and then she led the way out from behind their cover and across the wharf toward the *Quintana Roo*. The creaking of both ship and dock would cover any sound their tread might make, but she still moved as quietly as possible. Moments passed before Willow and Giles emerged from the ruined warehouse and then they were hurrying to the bottom of the gangplank to meet up with Buffy and the others.

The Slayer led them up the gangplank. Xander still carried the pillowcase she had insisted he bring, but Buffy took it from him now. Though they tried to be quiet, feet on metal were bound to make noise. Still, she expected that any sounds would be attributed to the sentries rather than intruders. Camazotz had trained his Kakchiquels to be fearless, but that had made them arrogant as well.

The deck of the old cargo vessel was deserted. Buffy raised a hand and gestured for Xander, Anya and Giles to go to the opposite side of the deck, and she stood with Willow and Oz until the others had taken their position. She handed Oz the pillowcase and he removed its contents, a dozen small round balls whose long wicks had been meticulously tied together. Buffy slipped a hand into her pocket and gave him the silver lighter she had brought.

Then she notched another arrow in her bow.

Again, she whistled. A shout would have brought vampires running. Instead, the whistle was meant to produce idle curiosity. After a moment, when there was no response at all, she whistled once more. To the fore and aft there were doors leading belowdecks. From what Willow had determined of this class of merchant ship, one led to the galley and crew's quarters and the other to the cargo hold.

Finally, a Kakchiquel face emerged from the door on

the left. Giles was nearest and he fired the crossbow the moment he had a clear shot. The vampire exploded in a cloud of ash. Another appeared seconds later from the cargo bay door and Willow took him out. Buffy had seen the power of her compound bow and so she held off, not wanting to make too much noise.

Over the course of the next several minutes, five other Kakchiquels were dusted in that fashion. During that time, Buffy could see Xander fidgeting impatiently. Nine dead. There was no way to know how many more of Camazotz's lackeys there were, and even a long, loud whistle brought no further inquiries. Buffy shot a glance at Giles across the deck and he nodded once.

The Slayer pointed toward the galley door to indicate that they should watch it, then she gestured for Oz to light the massive twined wick on the bouquet of colorful smoke bombs Xander had left over from the last Fourth of July. Buffy kept her bow aimed at the cargo bay door and nodded. Oz left his ax on the deck and ran, the twist of wicks sparking and hissing. He threw the smoke bombs down the stairs and into the hold.

Buffy held her breath.

They did not have long to wait. Cries of alarm rose from below as the smoke began to spread. Those shouts were followed by a horrible screeching and a flurry of hundreds of small, leathery wings. A few bats emerged almost immediately, wings beating the air furiously, and then the rest followed in a dark cloud of vermin.

Across the deck, even in the dark, Buffy could see the anxious expression on Giles's face. The others all stood at the ready, fearful of the bats. Behind her, Oz lit a package of firecrackers and threw them, fuse hissing, to the deck. The bats had begun to circle above, angry and curious and at least partially driven by the sinister intentions of their god, Camazotz.

The firecrackers began to explode. At Buffy's side, Willow flinched. The bats screeched again and fluttered off into the darkness over the ocean in search of quieter places to roost.

But they were the least of Buffy's concerns.

Even as the firecrackers popped and tiny explosions echoed off into the night, the battle began in earnest. Kakchiquels raced up from the cargo hold, their tattooed features contorted in the hideous visage of the vampire. They did not have to breathe and so the smoke was more a nuisance than an actual problem, but they were to protect their master and so they burst out onto the deck in a murderous rage.

More spilled from the opposite door, ascending from the crew's quarters. Six, ten, fifteen. Far more than Buffy would have thought were still aboard. The Slayer cursed under her breath and shot an arrow through the heart of the nearest vampire. It punched right through him and he exploded as if shattered into burning embers. The arrow tore through the shoulder of the Kakchiquel behind him, who shrieked in pain and surprise.

The ship rolled ponderously on the undulating ocean; the cold sea breeze blew across the deck. Under the starlight, the melee took on a surreal atmosphere, as though this were a secret war fought on the edge of some twilight borderland between reality and nightmare. In a way, Buffy thought that was correct.

There came a moment of stillness, when all was silent save for the ringing of a buoy out on the water and the distant screech of bats high in the air. Then the Kakchiquels began the low chant in their ancient language that had so unnerved Buffy once before. This time, she ignored it.

Another arrow flew, another vampire dusted. All around her, the conflict raged. Willow fired the crossbow at a scarred female Kakchiquel in a dirty linen shirt. The bolt caught in the flapping linen and the vampire descended upon Willow, but Oz stepped in and beheaded the creature before she could lay a hand on the witch.

The combat spread out across the deck. Giles used his crossbow and another Kakchiquel was dust, but then it was torn from his hands. Xander and Anya were forced to defend themselves and they hacked gracelessly at their attackers.

A half-naked vampire with gleaming bronze skin leaped at Buffy, eyes glittering with orange sparks. The Slayer had drawn another arrow from her quiver but had no time to use it. Instead she cracked the vampire across the head with the compound bow. It staggered back, disoriented from the force of the blow, and Buffy used that opportunity to slip up to it and drive the arrow into its chest with a single thrust.

Another was dust.

Still, there were at least nine left, and her friends were not faring too well now. As she glanced around, she saw that they were barely holding their own. Staying alive.

Buffy dropped the bow and pulled the sword from the scabbard across her back. Oz and Willow were faring all right and so she sprinted across the deck toward a cluster of vampires who were menacing the others. Xander slashed at one of them, tore it open from throat to belly, but his attack left him vulnerable. Even as Buffy raced toward him the others drove him down. Anya screamed, but Buffy could not make out the words through the noise of her own furious shouting.

A desperate terror was in Anya's wide eyes and the ocean wind blew her hair back as she brought the scimitar down again and again, hacking at the neck and shoulders of one of the vampires trying to dismember her boyfriend. But the ex-demon was just a human girl now and did not have the physical strength to cut the head off a Kakchiquel.

Giles kicked one of them in the head and as it began to look up, he grabbed its hair in one hand and a fistful of its clothes in the other and propelled it over the side of the boat to splash in the ocean below.

The vampire Anya had been bludgeoning thundered his pain and fury and rounded on her. But even as he lunged for the other girl, Buffy swung her blade in a clean, horizontal arc that sliced through his neck with a wet crunch. Through its dust, she saw Giles haul one of the vampires off Xander, who struggled with another, his sword already buried in its gut, the tip protruding from the vampire's back.

Buffy was about to go to his aid when she glanced at Anya and saw the way the girl's face had blanched.

"Uh-oh," Anya said, eyes wide.

Buffy turned away from the battle just as Camazotz emerged from the cargo hold in a crouch. A dark, sickly orange energy crackled all about his body, leaking from his eyes and from the slash in his chest where Willow had attacked him. His green, pock-marked flesh looked black in the starlight and as he unfolded his body and stood to his full height—easily eleven or twelve feet—Buffy could only imagine how horrifyingly magnificent he would have been at the peak of his strength. The god of bats, the prince of shadows.

"Slayer," the demon-god rasped as he sneered at her. His long tongue slithered out over the rows of razor teeth in his mouth and his piggish nose glistened wetly. His beard and hair were filthy and matted, and she thought he had never looked so primitive. Power radiated from him as though he had ripped a tear in the fabric of reality, a conduit into the demon dimension of his birth. With the exception of his mangled wings and the wound across his chest, Buffy thought this must be the primal visage of the god of bats that had terrified the Mayans into worshiping him in the first place.

The wind died.

The air erupted with ear-piercing screeches as the bats began to return.

With her left hand, Buffy reached behind her back and slipped a stake out of the small sheath in her waist-band. She glanced over at Willow and Oz. A pair of Kakchiquels menaced them, but all of the combatants in the melee on the deck of the *Quintana Roo* seemed to have frozen with Camazotz's arrival.

"Willow!" Buffy snapped.

Then she threw the stake so that it struck the deck and rolled up to Willow's feet. The witch snatched it up and stared at Buffy.

"Now would be good," Buffy told her.

Shaking her head with uncertainty, Willow held the stake in both hands and whispered something too quietly for Buffy to hear. Nothing happened. Then the bats began to descend and Willow screamed as they dove at her. She tried to slap them away as one of them became tangled in her hair. Oz batted several away from his own head.

The Kakchiquels began to move in.

"Plan B!" Willow screamed.

*No*, Buffy thought. *You can do this.*

But she had no choice now. With sword in hand Buffy raced at Camazotz. The demon-god lashed out with a long arm and struck her in the temple. Buffy went down, rolled across the deck and was up again as Camazotz reached for her. She ducked and shot a straight kick up into the raw place on his abdomen where his Kakchiquels suckled for his power. Camazotz cried out at this blow to such a tender area, and she knew then that he was vulnerable.

"You hide it well, Camazotz, but you belong on the Mayan pantheon's injured reserve list," Buffy said, staring at the demon-god as he snorted hot, fetid breath in her face.

Buffy leaped into a high spin and brought her leg

around in a kick to the bat-god's filthy bearded jaw. Several of his teeth broke and Camazotz howled in pain.

"You were a crappy husband and the wife Bobbitted your wings, then took off," she said, filled with loathing for this creature. "You should've let her run. Left her alone."

Leathery wings fluttered around Buffy, a bat tore at her hair and scalp. Buffy slapped a few away and ignored the rest, even as one of them tore tiny claws into her neck. Camazotz tried to reach for her, but he was staggering and Buffy was too fast for him. She ducked inside his reach and drove the sword deep into the wound Willow had already made, then twisted the blade and tugged it upward, tearing whatever passed for organs inside an ancient demon-lord.

Camazotz roared and stumbled backward.

Buffy tore the sword out of him and sliced two bats into pieces as they flew toward her. She ripped one off her neck and stamped on it. Around her, she heard the shouts of her friends, still alive, still fighting, but she could not take the time to turn and check on them.

For Camazotz had climbed to his feet, one taloned hand clamped over his bleeding wound. Weakly, he lifted his other hand and pointed at her, sparks jumping from one claw to another. Buffy had seen him use his demonic power before. Whether it was magickal or something innate in him, she did not know. But it mattered not. As a stream of dark electrical fire arced from his hand, Buffy leaped from its path and the deck of the ship was seared and charred where it struck.

But Camazotz nearly collapsed from the effort.

Buffy raised her sword and started for him, ready to finish the job.

The demon-god raised his eyes. "That you have brought me to this is shameful, for my Kakchiquels are like my children. But Camazotz must survive, and you, Slayer, must be destroyed."

The malformed, withered wings on his back seemed to flutter as though he were trying to fly. Then Camazotz reached his hand out again. Dark fire rippled all over him and leaked from his eyes, but instead of power erupting from his fingers, the reverse happened. The six Kakchiquels who remained alive froze, all of them screaming in agony simultaneously as thin tendrils of orange lightning shot from their bodies and into that of their master. They jittered as though electrocuted.

Then, as one, they dusted.

The ocean wind blew, carrying the remains of Camazotz's minions away over the waves.

Above, the bats shrieked and flew off again, seemingly now freed from their god's control.

On the deck, Anya and Xander helped an exhausted, bleeding Giles. Oz embraced Willow as their adrenaline subsided, the fear that they were all about to die giving way to sudden relief. It was quiet, almost as though it were over. And they all seemed to think it was.

Then, one by one, they all turned toward Buffy. Looked at her, then past her.

Buffy knew it was not over.

Whatever of his power had been siphoned by those

surviving Kakchiquels had been drawn back into Camazotz. The god of bats stood tall again now and his entire
body seemed bathed in a crackling orange glow. His
mouth hung open in a perpetual hiss, eyes raw balls of
fire in his skull. The demon's hair and beard were stiff
and standing on end with the electric aura of magick
surrounding him.

Worst of all, Camazotz's wounds were gone, and
though they were still vestigial and worthless for actual
flying, his wings seemed more whole now, less withered. They moved slowly on his back as if in rhythm
with his breathing. The dark god moved with reptilian
grace and swiftness, swaying in anticipation as he
stalked across the deck of the *Quintana Roo*. His foot-
falls seemed to shake the ship.

In her peripheral vision, Buffy saw the others begin to
move, to race toward Camazotz to aid her.

"Stop!" she snapped.

They all paused.

"Buffy, you need our help," Giles insisted.

Camazotz laughed at that, the sound like the slither-
ing of cobras.

"I need you alive," Buffy told him, deadly earnest.

"Are we back to that again?" he asked.

"No," she replied, as calmly as she was able. "But
there are still times you all have to stand aside. Back off,
right now."

There was a moment's pause in which Camazotz
slowly moved toward her, watching them all with dark
curiosity.

"The only thing you can do for them now, Slayer, is die first," the demon told her.

Buffy held the sword out to one side and ran at him. Long before she would have reached the demon-god, she leaped high into an aerial somersault that took her a dozen feet off the deck of the ship. Without a weapon of gold there was always the chance he might return for her, but she could still destroy him. The sword whipped around and she slashed the blade down toward Camazotz's skull. Had it connected, it would have split his head in two.

Like a serpent, Camazotz dodged to one side. His arms shot up and snatched Buffy from the air. One hand clutched her throat and the other wrapped around her right arm at the bicep. The Slayer jittered with the dark, draining surge of demonic power that shot through her when Camazotz touched her. Her teeth clamped together and pain lanced through her body, making her arms and legs shake. Buffy dangled upside down far above the deck of the ship. She snatched the sword from her right hand and used her left arm to hack down at the god of bats again.

The blade bit deep into Camazotz's shoulder and only stopped when it hit bone.

With a cry of rage, the demon-god let go of her throat and knocked the blade from her hand. Still clutching her by the arm, he lifted her up, arms and legs splayed, and then slammed Buffy against the deck over and over as easily as if she were a rag doll. Something cracked in her teeth and she bit the inside of her mouth. Blood spilled across her lips, tasting of wet copper.

She could hear Giles and Willow screaming.

Her vision began to dim as she saw Xander rushing toward Camazotz with a sword upraised. She wanted to call to him to stay back but then she crashed to the deck again and her voice failed her. Camazotz swatted him away effortlessly and Xander rolled across the deck.

At last the demon-god simply hurled Buffy away. She struck her head as she landed. For several heartbeats, she blacked out. A second later, her vision cleared and Willow was kneeling above her, stake in hand. Even as Buffy began to sit up, her best friend began to intone a spell in French. Buffy made out the words for gold and fire, but that was all.

Then Willow started back as if someone had slapped her and the stake fell to the deck with a metallic clank.

It was made of gold.

"That was . . . I did . . . did you see that?" Willow asked excitedly.

Buffy lifted the heavy, pointed shaft of gold and shook herself to clear her head. She shot a sidelong glance at Willow.

"Thanks. Just what the Slayer ordered."

"But . . . how?" Willow asked.

Buffy grinned as she advanced toward Camazotz. "I think you're going to be amazed at what you're capable of."

She left the young witch standing there staring after her. Power still crackled in a sheath of lightning that emanated from Camazotz's body. Buffy ached down to her bones, her head felt like her skull was splintered in pieces and there were bloody scrapes all across her face.

All it did was piss her off.

Again, Camazotz darted his head back and forth as she moved in toward him. Buffy held the stake down along one leg, careful not to let the demon-god see it. She stepped even closer, but what she truly wanted was to draw him out; she was not about to make the first move again. Buffy closed in, watching, waiting for him to strike this time.

"You face me unarmed?" Camazotz asked. "You rush to your death."

"Why not?" Buffy asked. "Time to put an end to this thing."

With a hiss of fetid breath and a flutter of bony wings, he swayed to the left and then darted in at her from that side.

Buffy barely sidestepped; his talons slashed her side. She grabbed his arm with her left hand and hauled him closer, pulled him down to her level. Her right hand flashed up and she buried the heavy gold spike in one of those burning orange eyes. There was a popping noise as she pulled the stake out.

Camazotz screamed and clapped his clawed hands across his face.

The Slayer sprang at him, wrapped her legs around his torso and rode him backward. With both hands, she stabbed the sharp length of gold through his chest and pierced his demonic heart.

When she landed on the deck on top of Camazotz, he was already dead.

# EPILOGUE

Knees weak, Buffy nearly buckled as she climbed to her feet. She took a long breath to steady herself and stared down at the corpse of the prince of the Mayan underworld.

His eyes were sunken pits now, one of them cored out by the golden stake. The energy that had burned like an inferno within him was gone now, dissipated into the ether or drawn back into whatever nether realm spawned him. But Camazotz was dead, and if the scribblings of a vampire despot who would now never exist were to be believed, the god of bats was destroyed once and for all.

The dead thing had already begun to wither.

Buffy turned her back on Camazotz to see Xander retrieving her compound bow and Oz picking up pieces of a shattered crossbow. Giles, Anya and Willow stood watching Buffy as she walked toward them.

As she approached, a bruised and bloodied Giles

smiled tiredly at her. Buffy went to him and hugged him tightly.

"Ow!" he said sharply. "Cracked rib, I think. If not before, then certainly now."

The man shifted awkwardly, perhaps a little uncomfortable with such an obvious show of affection from her. Buffy did not care. A thousand things went through her mind, feelings she wanted to convey about what he meant to her and how it had tormented her to see him so horribly transformed in that dark future.

Instead she just smiled up at him. "We make a good team," she said. "All of us."

When she stepped back Giles swayed a bit as though he might need her to lean on, but then he straightened up again. "I confess I feared the worst earlier tonight," he said. "In the harbor master's office, I mean. You ought to have run, you know. Left me behind. He'd likely have left me alive as a negotiating tool. The first rule of slaying is—"

"Don't die," Buffy finished for him. "I know. But sometimes you have to break the rules."

"Excuse me!" Xander said loudly as he and Oz strode over, both of their arms laden with weapons. "Not that I want to interrupt the hey-look-we're-alive mushy moment, but how 'bout some rousing applause instead? 'Cause I'm thinkin' we were a well-oiled machine. We opened the industrial-size can of vampire whup-ass tonight, and it was a double-header! We were spectacular."

"Songs will be sung of it," Oz observed solemnly.

"We were the magnificent six!" Xander added.

Oz raised an eyebrow. "Weren't there seven?"

Xander was indignant. "Not tonight."

"Ah." Oz nodded sagely.

Buffy smiled. This was how it was supposed to be. Xander alive and laughing, Anya at his side. Oz with eyes wise and kind instead of wild. Giles, Willow, all of them together. Buffy thought that soon she might have to make a call down to Los Angeles, just to hear Angel's voice. She might not speak, might just hang up, but she would know he was there.

"We *were* pretty amazing," she agreed. "Thanks, you guys. Really. You all really came through."

Anya piped up brightly. "I was nearly killed many times and even helped save Xander's life. I was an asset. I still feel strangely exhilarated by our triumph."

"You were great," Buffy assured her. "You all were. And Willow gets the MVP for pulling off the magick trick Giles didn't believe existed."

Giles blinked and began to protest.

"Ah, it was nothing," Willow said with a broad grin. Then her expression faltered. "Hang on."

As they all watched, she went to the decaying corpse of the ancient demon-god. With both hands, Willow tugged the golden stake free of his chest cavity. She flinched as though he might come back to life but Camazotz was truly dead. Willow went to the far side of the deck and dropped the heavy gold spike overboard. They all heard the splash as it hit the water and sank immediately to the bottom.

"All right, now who's acting like a crazy person?"

Xander protested. "Will, what the heck was that? Do you have any idea how much that thing is probably worth?"

"That's the rule," Willow replied, eyes ticking toward Buffy and then back to Xander. "Alchemy only works if you have no thought of personal gain."

"Well, that sucks," Xander said. "Who made that rule?"

Buffy shivered, the words familiar, an echo of a future that would never be. Her gaze lingered on Xander and Anya then as they stood with their arms around one another and a lightness that was nearly giddy swept through her.

It was an echo, but that was all. That future was gone forever now, impossible. Anna and August might never become Slayers. It existed only in her memories. The memories had begun to dim, but they did not leave her. Buffy would not let herself forget, for she never wanted to take what she had for granted again. For a short time she had thought that in order to achieve contentment and still fulfill her duties, she had to split herself in two, separate Buffy Summers from the Slayer. But she knew now that without all the things that made Buffy Summers unique, and all the people who cared about her, the Slayer could not survive.

Together, leaning on one another for strength, carrying weapons which now seemed so much heavier than before, they left the *Quintana Roo* and trudged along the wharf back to where they had parked. Buffy lagged behind, not because she was more tired than they were, but because she was watching them.

Willow noticed and dropped back to walk beside her.

"You have an awful lot of explaining to do, you know," the young witch said.

Buffy smiled. "I'm sorry I've been cryptic. If it's okay with you, though, I don't really want to go into it too much. Let's just say I had a vision . . . a kind of prophecy, I guess. That's how I knew what I knew."

"How much of it came true?" Willow asked.

The others had gotten even farther ahead. Buffy cast a sidelong glance at her, studied Willow closely. It was a long moment before she replied.

"Only the good parts," Buffy replied. "You know, you're quite the witch."

Willow linked her arm with Buffy's. "You're not so bad yourself. But—and not that I'm knocking it—when did you become Positive-Outlook-Girl?"

Buffy laughed softly. "We're alive, Will. That could change at any time, but right now? We're alive. If we're careful, and we plan ahead, and we back each other up, I think we can stay that way."

They walked on in silence then and rejoined the others in front of Oz's van. It occurred to Buffy that the life she had just described to Willow—a life of constant war, with the ever-present threat of attack from the forces of darkness—was hardly the brightest she could imagine.

But it would do.

After what she had seen, it would do just fine.

## THE END

# About the Author

CHRISTOPHER GOLDEN is the award-winning, *L.A. Times* best-selling author of such novels as *Straight on 'Til Morning, Strangewood, Prowlers,* and the *Body of Evidence* series of teen thrillers.

Golden has also written a great many books and comic books related to the TV series *Buffy the Vampire Slayer* and *Angel.* His other comic book work includes stories featuring such characters as Batman, Wolverine, Spider-Man, The Crow, and Hellboy, among many others.

As a pop culture journalist, he was the editor of the Bram Stoker Award–winning book of criticism, *CUT!: Horror Writers on Horror Film,* and co-author of both *Buffy the Vampire Slayer: The Monster Book* and *The Stephen King Universe.*

Golden was born and raised in Massachusetts, where he still lives with his family. He graduated from Tufts

University. He is currently at work on the third book in the *Prowlers* series, *Predator and Prey,* and a new novel for Signet called *The Ferryman.* There are more than four million copies of his books in print. Please visit him at www.christophergolden.com.

While helping a friend search for her lost brother, Buffy is drawn into a dangerous web of intrigue. Meanwhile Giles and the rest of the Scoobs are on the trail of a shadow stalker—a trail that leads straight to the city of Angels....

Someone is kidnapping the children of the rich and powerful and sending them off to another plane. With the lives of the kidnapped teens and one dangerously talented young woman at stake, Buffy and Angel venture off into the uncharted dimension to do battle....

# UNSEEN

An epic trilogy that crosses the lives of Buffy, Angel, and their respective cohorts as they battle the forces of evil....

### #1-The Burning
### #2-Door to Alternity
### #3-Long Way Home
### By Nancy Holder and Jeff Mariotte

**Published by Pocket Books**

# Everyone's got his demons....

# ANGEL™

**If it takes an eternity,
he will make amends.**

❖

Original stories based
on the TV show
Created by Joss Whedon
& David Greenwalt

Available from Pocket Pulse
Published by Pocket Books